The Raids

MICK LOWE

The Raids

THE NICKEL RANGE TRILOGY • VOLUME 1

Baraka
Books

Montréal

ISBN 978-1-77186-012-3 pbk; 978-1-77186-017-8 epub; 978-1-77186-018-5 pdf; 978-1-77186-019-2 mobi/kindle

Cover painting, "Hardrock," back cover illustration "The Siege of the Mine Mill Local 598 Hall" by Oryst Sawchuk
Cover by Folio infographie
All illustrations by Oryst Sawchuk
Book design by Folio infographie

Legal Deposit, 2nd quarter 2014
Bibliothèque et Archives nationales du Québec
Library and Archives Canada

Published by Baraka Books of Montreal
6977, rue Lacroix
Montréal, Québec H4E 2V4
Telephone: 514 808-8504
info@barakabooks.com
www.barakabooks.com

Printed and bound in Quebec

Baraka Books acknowledges the generous support of its publishing program from the Société de développement des entreprises culturelles du Québec (SODEC) and the Canada Council for the Arts.

Canada Council for the Arts

We acknowledge the financial support of the Government of Canada, through the National Translation Program for Book Publishing for our translation activities and through the Canada Book Fund (CBF) for our publishing activities.

Trade Distribution & Returns
Canada and the United States Independent Publishers Group
1-800-888-4741 (IPG1);
orders@ipgbook.com

Contents

For Anita, through it all,
-Still my Sky.
-Still your Slim.

AUTHOR'S NOTE: *The Raids* is a work of fiction, based on actual events that occurred in my adopted hometown, Sudbury, Ontario, at the height of the Cold War, well within the living memory of many mature Sudburians...

The author anticipates the reader will inevitably be tempted to ask: "Did this really happen?" To which the author will reply "This is a work of fiction, and besides, you're asking the wrong question, rather than the right one: 'Could this actually have happened?'"

To which the author replies, "Emphatically, yes."

Although I have taken liberties with time—compressing many actual events of the raids, which lasted for half a decade in the 1960s, into a single year.

No one actually died during the Steel raids—or, rather, no such murders were ever reported during this turbulent time. However...

All characters appearing in this work are fictitious. Any resemblance to real persons, living or dead, is purely coincidental.

List of Illustrations
by Oryst Sawchuk

"Freakin' hard rock miners, I swear—
fix a watch with an axe and a wedge."

Rick Briggs, President
Mine Mill Local 598
1984-1995

"Eisenhower, though, combined the mind-set of a
warrior with a sober understanding of the devastation
full-scale war brings. That led him to covert action.
With the Dulles brothers as his right and left arms,
he led the United States into a secret global
conflict that raged throughout his presidency.

"In the secrecy-shrouded 1950s and for long after-
ward, the scope of this unseen war remained obscure.
Truths about it have emerged slowly, episodically
in isolated pieces over the course of decades. Woven
back together in their original sequence,
they tell an illuminating tale."

-Stephen Kinzer, *The Brothers: John Foster Dulles,
Allen Dulles, and their Secret World War* (2013)

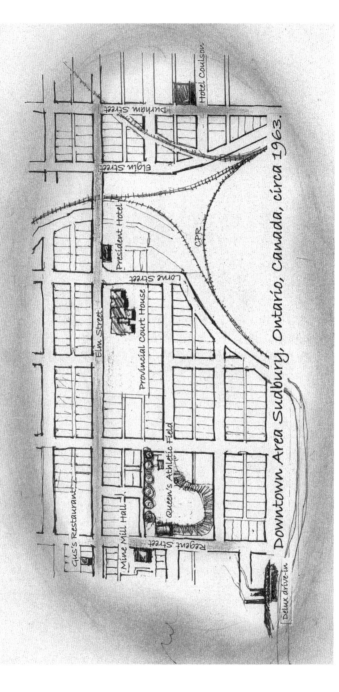

Downtown Area Sudbury, Ontario, Canada, circa 1963.

PART ONE

Jake, Ascending

1

Jake, Ascending

Dayshift, Garson Mine
Sudbury, Ontario, Canada
Monday, May 6, 1963
6 AM

What they neglected to tell him before that first shift was that you weren't lowered into the mine; you were dropped.

The only inkling of the bullet-like descent of the cage, packed with its human cargo, plummeting down the greased shaft guides, was the build-up of pressure on Jake's eardrums. The miners were packed so tightly, in fact, that there was no room for Jake and his forty-five or so compatriots to carry their lunch boxes. Instead, each man simply placed his lunch box between his boots on the splintered wooden floor of the cage.

The air was redolent of excessive aftershave and explosive Cold War tension. When the cage was between levels it was deceptively quiet, with little indication of the colossal forces at play around their peaceful, gently rocking world: the cage rocketing downward toward the molten centre of the earth at a hundred feet per second, suspended from a tightly wound, heavily greased wire rope thousands of feet long unspooling with unimaginable rapidity. Only when the cage passed a level—its bright lights and promise of life appearing and disappearing in the blink of an eye—was there a sense of the speed of their descent.

"He's a fuckin' Commie," Jake heard from someone standing in front of him.

"*Câlice!*" The French invective was hurled from the back of the cage.

"Oh, and Thibault's Red, too."

"*Tabernac!*" again from the rear.

There wasn't enough room to swing a cat, much less a punch, which was a good thing, too, Jake reflected, as the cage glided to a halt. With a rapid insouciance born of countless repetitions the cage tender yanked on his bell cord a few times, raised the scissors gate and swung out the heavy steel gate, the signal at once reaching the hoistman on surface nearly a half-mile above just after he braked the cage to a stop, the heavy car bobbing slightly as the wire rope slackened and tightened to absorb the strain.

"Twenty-two hundred, gentlemen," announced the tender with a wry, courtly formality.

They crowded out onto the level, still tightly bunched, like a school of fish. Instinctively Jake glanced down before he stepped out of the cage. Its floor was nearly flush with the deck. This was a wizardry that would come to profoundly impress Jake: how the hoistman, sitting in his easy chair in his silent, dimly lit little antechamber adjacent to the shaft house and equipped only with a few manual levers, foot pedals and a giant circular glass-enclosed dial, could so unerringly calibrate the forces of gravity and momentum over a distance of a half-mile through solid rock.

He stepped out onto the level.

And then a half-dozen novel sensations washed over Jake in a rush: the hollow loud metallic clang as the tender pulled the heavy gate shut, the ear-splitting ring of the hoist signal bells, the underground smells of a working hard rock mine—the damp most of all, suffused with the hint of sulphur overpowered by the acrid reek of ammonia.

Jake was surprised how light it was—not bright, certainly, but here at the loading station there were a half-dozen bulbs glowing inside protective steel frames. The walls had been sprayed with some kind of reflective coating. Off in the distance down the main haulage drift a string of lights burned bravely in a losing battle against the all enveloping dark. The world ended abruptly past the last one.

Even as he was taking his bearings, Jake became aware of a slender older man of medium height standing facing the shaft.

"You young McCool?" the face behind the question broke into a ready, welcoming smile above an outstretched hand. "I knew your dad. We were stewards together at Stobie. Big Bill was a good union man. I'm Bob Jesperson, your new partner."

Jake accepted the proffered hand. The grip was firm, but not bone-crushing.

"Pleased to meet you, Mr. Jesperson."

The older man waved the formality aside.

"Please, let's make it Bob."

Jake studied the older man, found a friendly face and clear blue eyes just visible behind a pair of eyeglasses surrounded by the safety glasses which were a mandatory piece of protective equipment for everyone in the mine. Jesperson turned to face the haulage drift before looking up at Jake, who stood a good head taller than the older man.

"Ever been underground before?"

Jake shook his head.

Jesperson turned his back to the shaft and pointed down the tunnel, which was the only exit from the loading station.

"Haulage drift. Main drift. Muck's trammed out on those rails you see there"—for the first time Jake noticed the narrow gauge rails on the floor of the drift—"to be hoisted to surface."

Jake nodded. Jesperson motioned for him to follow and set off down the drift.

II

Was, Jake thought, as he trudged along behind Bob. His dad *was* a good union man, fairly worshipping at the altar of the Great, Almighty Mine Mill, until the disastrous strike of '58 had nearly ruined the family, and the seemingly impregnable Local 598 along with it. The bargaining agent for all of International Nickel's eighteen thousand production and maintenance workers in the Sudbury Basin, Local 598 was larger than many whole unions, a true trade union colossus.

Oh, it had all started well enough that fall in 1958, with a breezy confidence borne of hubris and inexperience. For the first fifteen years of its existence the big Local had negotiated a series of one-year agreements without ever striking, which had fostered prosperity, yes, but also false confidence as to the impacts of their actions: the winter alone would bring the company to its knees, with water lines in the surface plants freezing and bursting, and furnace linings cracking in the unaccustomed cold.

But the long post-war boom was finally, unimaginably, drawing to a close, and a mild recession was beginning. Demand for nickel slackened accordingly, and the world price was buoyed, paradoxically, only by their own strike.

As Christmas approached, bleak reality set in. Mine Mill, which had earlier been expelled from the AFL-CIO for its left-wing leanings, was unable to turn to other unions for financial support, with the singular exception of Jimmy Hoffa's Teamsters, which had also been expelled from the American house of labour years earlier. When a delegation of Sudbury strike leaders appealed to the Teamsters for support Hoffa himself greeted them warmly, pledging one million dollars in strike support on the spot. It was a generous enough gesture—one that would be all but unrecorded in history, but amongst eighteen thousand workers a million bucks didn't last long. Strike pay, minimal though it had been, was reduced to a trickle, and then dried up entirely. The strikers' wives, faced with the prospect of a Christmas without presents for their children, began to waver in their support of their husbands' cause, a hesitation that was quickly exploited by a right-wing mayor who organized a mass pre-Christmas, anti-strike wives' rally in the city's largest hockey arena.

The water lines in the plants did not freeze. Furnace linings did not crack. Instead, the company itself simply dug in, content to save millions in wages while selling stockpiled nickel at a slightly elevated world price.

Family savings dwindled and cupboards became bare just as the cold weather and holidays loomed. The McCools were no exception. Instead, they became gleaners. It was a humiliating act of desperation Jake would never forget: Big Bill, proud Mine Miller and highly paid, highly skilled hard rock miner, piled his whole family into their old black Chevy sedan for the trip to a farmer's field out in the Valley—the farmer was a union sympathizer who opened his fields to strikers—to dig up any unharvested potatoes they could pry out of the frozen ground. They unearthed the spuds with shovels and spades at first, before sinking to their knees to claw their quarry out of the frozen, unyielding earth with their bare hands and with fingers numbed by the cold.

Jake's mom did what she could, improvising dozens of new ways to cook potatoes, but there was no way to disguise the bitter taste of defeat that accompanied every meal that terrible winter. Still Big Bill, long a strong union man, clung stubbornly to his pride, exhorting his fellow strikers to greater resolve out on the picket lines. But at home, behind closed doors, the strain was almost more than any of them could bear.

And for what?

Jake still wondered as he trailed down the drift behind Bob Jesperson. The strike ended, finally, when the union had been forced to settle for the same offer it had rejected before the strike began, before the hardship, the near starvation, the barren Christmas. Even Jake's dad, proud Mine Miller though he'd been, had to admit it was a terrible defeat.

Shortly after the strike ended Big Bill McCool quietly slipped into the Union Hall and surrendered his steward's badge.

III

The strike's outcome cast a long shadow over the big Local's leadership. Blood was in the water, and the union's monthly membership meetings, always lively affairs, became downright fractious. In the wake of Mine Mill's expulsion from the AFL-CIO the United Steelworkers of America became the officially sanctioned industrial union in Mine Mill's historic jurisdiction, and the Pittsburgh-based Steelworkers had quickly begun to swell their own ranks by gobbling up, one by one, Mine Mill Locals in the States.

There were growing suspicions that Steel had now set its sights on the biggest prize of all—Local 598. Those fears were confirmed when Steel organizers began to sign Steelworkers' membership cards on the job, launching an all-out raid on the big Local. The insurgents were led by vocal opponents of the progressive leaders who had so badly bungled the strike, and the pro-Steel forces soon gained traction. The conflict quickly surged beyond the Union Hall to engulf the entire community. The city was split right down the middle: either you were a Mine Miller, and a suspected Commie dupe, or pro-Steel, and a McCarthyite tool of Washington and the CIA. There was no middle ground, nowhere to hide. On Sundays Roman Catholic priests inveighed from their pulpits against the Mine Mill, warning their flocks about the perils of godless Communism. There were Mine Mill bars, and Steelworker bars. Extremes played out in public, and among the innocents. In the schoolyards Steel kids ganged up on Mine Mill kids and vice versa. Fistfights between factions and, on bad days, full-on riots became commonplace. Global Cold War escalated into a heated local civil war on the streets of Sudbury.

Personally, Jake could care less. He had little use for unions, anyway. Oh, he conceded that they had probably been necessary when they were first organized, in the Dirty Thirties when everyone was out of work, and young men his age had been forced to hop freights, riding the rods all over Canada to seek employment. But this was the sixties; times had changed.

IV

They had long since passed the last light bulb in the drift, and Bob slowed his pace before turning to face Jake.

"Turn off your lamp," he ordered Jake.

Bob extinguished his own cap lamp, the battery-powered bulb clipped to his hard hat that was now his only source of illumination.

Jake followed suit, and quickly found himself enveloped in a total darkness he could never have imagined. There was no hint of light. No gleam, no glimmer, no shadow. It was as if the sun had never shone, and in this place never would. Instinctively, Jake waved his hand just in front of his nose. Nothing. He was disembodied. The effect was almost dizzying, and not altogether pleasant. The darkness was absolute, the new, all-pervading normal. Impenetrable. Eternal.

Point taken in a trice.

"Okay," Bob said simply before switching his lamp back on. Jake quickly followed suit, heartily grateful even for the dim yellow beams that barely pierced the dusty, mote-filled gloom.

They resumed their trek through the drift, Jesperson once again in the lead. It was hard going, even though the floor was nearly level. The cross-ties for the tram tracks were awkwardly spaced, either slightly more or slightly less than a grown man's step. The rails were inviting and fairly flat, but so greasy from the all-pervasive mine damp as to present yet another hazard. Nor was venturing off the rail bed an option—the ballasted right-of-way fell off sharply on either side to a ditch where brackish water had collected.

Jake found it a struggle to keep pace with his new partner, who forged ahead with the nonchalance of a man out for a casual, if brisk, Sunday stroll.

Even though he was only nineteen, Jake was surprised, and more than a little irritated, at the exertion he felt in keeping up to the much older man. Why, he was even working up a sweat, and felt slightly winded! Much of it, Jake rationalized, stemmed from his unfamiliar attire.

Heavy, ill-fitting miner's boots—steel-toed and steel-shanked—cumbersome thick webbed safety belt, heavy battery strapped to heavy belt, rubberized cable from battery to cap lamp, all combined to weigh him down, to hamper his movement so that even the simplest motion demanded extra effort.

Jake felt sheepish, and more than a little alarmed, at this revelation of his own vulnerability. For as long as he could remember he'd always been the biggest, toughest kid on the block. He'd inherited his father's frame, if not—yet—his bulk, which meant he now packed more than two hundred pounds of lean muscle onto a frame well over six feet. But his very size had made him the target of every would-be schoolyard bully in every class. The inevitable confrontations invariably ended in blood and tears— though rarely Jake's own. Possessor of a dangerous, quick temper, Jake loved a good scrap, even though it usually meant being hauled to the principal's office despite what had been, to him, self-evident acts of self-defence.

Hockey had been a salvation. Jake loved the speed of the game, the violence of the corners. He developed into a serviceable defenceman with a surprisingly wicked point shot which made him a staple penalty killer. And he never minded dropping the gloves, either. Here at last was a place where he could surrender to the red eye of his temper without hindrance. In fact, his coach and teammates and the crowd—especially the crowd—went crazy when Jake pummeled his opponent nearly senseless and blood began to spatter on the ice. Besides being a safe outlet for his temper, Jake's on-ice abilities had also helped him stay in school, transforming him into a hero, at least for the first two years of high school.

But during his junior year Jake had run afoul of a demanding trigonometry teacher backed by an iron-willed principal who was determined to put a stop to his shenanigans. Jake was heartily indifferent to the expulsion notice when it came—school had always been, at best, barely tolerable.

"Uh, Bob?" Jake directed his query at the back of his new partner.

"Bob?" Jake repeated, a little louder this time.

Still no answer. Oh well, perhaps it was just as well. Jake felt foolish about his question, which would have been "Are we nearly there yet?" Even to Jake it felt like something a peevish child would ask his parents on an over-long road trip.

Maybe the old fellow was a little hard of hearing ... It was something Jake had also noticed with his own father and uncles, miners all, especially when they gathered around the kitchen table over beer, recounting endless rounds drilled and blasted, copious tons of muck hoisted, the rascality of diverse shift bosses, many now long since retired. They were all slightly on the deaf side, big men with booming voices, each eager to make himself heard, so as the beer flowed and the night wore on and the winter windows steamed up, the din in the McCools' cramped kitchen began to rival that of the stormy end of a production heading itself. Jake's mother and her sisters-in-law retreated to the relative tranquility of the living room before the re-enactment of these prodigious mining feats ever began, but Jake sat cross-legged on the kitchen floor, soaking up every word. The Romance of Mining.

Bob came to a stop next to a short tunnel branching off at a right angle from the haulage drift.

"1050 cross-cut," he gestured.

Jake could make out a few cap lamps, and a few forms moving about around a piece of noisy equipment.

"See how those fellas are wearing their lights on their shoulders?"

Bob was yelling now, directly into Jake's ear. "They're shifters! Only shift bosses do that! So when you see 'em coming, look sharp! Always have your safety gear on whenever they're around, or else they'll give ya a Step, right? And for Chrissake don't ever let 'em catch ya drillin' a bootleg!"

Jake nodded. He knew from the kitchen table talk that Steps were punishment meted out by company supervisors for on-the-job policy infractions. A Step One was a relatively light penalty, but a Step Five meant outright dismissal. A "bootleg" he was less certain about.

"And if you ever see any of 'em running like hell outta the mine, like they're scared shitless, ignore 'em, you understand me?"

Jake nodded again.

The pair resumed their trek.

After another few paces, Bob paused again.

"1052 cross-cut." Again he motioned to a short perpendicular tunnel.

Again Jake could make out a few figures moving about, the dim illumination of cap lamps, but this time there was no noise.

"Samplers and engineers," Bob explained in his normal speaking voice. "And if you ever see *them* running outta the mine like they're scared shitless, ignore them, too, understand?"

Jake nodded, and they resumed their trek.

At length Bob led the way off the drift.

"This here's our heading."

Jake sensed they were leaving a well-travelled road and entering a space that was alien, unexplored and alluring. And more than a little dangerous. Gone was the level ground of the haulage drift, with its capacious, smoothly arched roof.

Now, suddenly, they were clambering through and around a tricky surface littered by small jagged rocks that were sometimes the size of small boulders.

Finally Bob stopped after they entered what appeared to Jake to be a vast, yawning cavern.

"This here's our stope. It's where we make our money."

"How's the ground, Bob?" Jake was already instinctively shining his lamp up to inspect the roof of the place. He could make out chunks of rock, some nearly the size of those Beetles the Volkswagen company was just beginning to sell so many of. The rocks, which had evidently worked loose from the roof of the stope, were rendered harmless by a heavy wire mesh screen. Jake didn't even want to think about the damage they could do if they were to fall on him or Bob.

Jesperson shrugged. "Oh, so-so. Garson's an old mine, so it's loosened up a good bit. We're mining out the pillars now."

"How … How's the bonus, Bob?"

"Well now, that's gonna depend on how good a driller you turn out to be. Ready to get to work?"

Jake nodded, and Bob walked to one end of the stope, a wall that was partly covered with garish white painted markings, which Bob pointed at. "This here's the face, what we call the breast. These marks were put here by the engineers to show us just where to drill. Our job is to drill off a round, holes eight feet deep, load them and take out our round, before afternoon shift comes in."

Jake nodded that he understood.

"Well, let's get at 'er then … Here, you'll be needin' this."

Bob proffered a medium-sized adjustable open-end crescent wrench. "You can fix most anything with one of these. And if all else fails you can always use it as a hammer. Mind, now, everything turns backward in a mine. Counter-clockwise, right? Everything is threaded so it turns to the left."

Bob surveyed the breast, playing the beam from his cap lamp across it, before beginning to use it as a pointer. Like a schoolteacher standing in front of a blackboard, Jake thought.

The dim yellow beam swept over the four topmost painted circles, which formed an arc. "Back holes," Bob explained. "Back's what we call the roof of a stope, or heading."

Below the back-hole painted marks Jake could make out five more marks, also forming a rainbow below the top four. Beneath that was a dense cluster of marks inside a square. "This here's our cut," Bob said, indicating the cluster. His light swept over the bottom three marks in a horizontal line that formed the bottom of the square. "These are your helpers." Next the light played down across the four bottom marks that were just above the floor of the stope. "And these are your lifters. When it comes time to blast we wire 'em all just so with the igniter cord so each shot goes in the right order. That way we get a nice clean round, see?"

Jake nodded, even though the strange markings and sudden welter of information might as well have been so many Egyptian hieroglyphics. Bob's light rose again, this time to a spot on the breast where there were no marks, nothing that Jake could see. The light stopped at a slight discolouration in the rock. Jake could just make out the faint outline of a circle. "Bootleg," Bob warned. "Unexploded powder, where the cross-shift's helpers didn't all quite blow."

Bob's light wiggled all across the breast again. "See all that glitter?"

Jake nodded.

"That there's free gold, free silver. Very rare you ever see that, but this here's a very high grade stope. They say just the PMs—the precious metals—'ll pay for the nickel in muck this rich. You don't see it every day, that's for sure. High grade's soft ground. Easier to drill, but also a lot less stable. Ya gotta be careful 'bout ground conditions."

Bob knelt to pick up a piece of equipment, grunting as he stood back up. "Jackleg drill."

Jake studied the apparatus cradled in Bob's arms. Two black rubberized hoses trailed from it. The whole affair was heavy and unwieldy, that much was evident. It was basically two pieces, the leg, which telescoped in and out of a piston, and the drill itself, which were joined at a pivot point where Bob was standing. The piston was roughly five feet long, and the drill steel, which was notched into the front of the drill, protruded for another six feet or so. Balance and leverage were the thing, as Jake could plainly see. Bob hefted the mechanism into place.

"Ready?"

Jake nodded.

Bob pulled up on a lever at the back of the drill—the throttle—and pointed the tip of the drill steel at the exact centre of one of the white painted markings.

The jackleg, which had been an inert piece of metal weighing well in excess of one hundred pounds, dead weight, now sprang alarmingly to life. The air line, which provided the motive force at one hundred pounds per square inch of pressure, stiffened and hissed, the piston extended the leg to its full length and the drill steel started to gush water from its tip as it began to smash against the face.

The device was now a living, powerful thing, instantly alive with an ear-splitting roar. A jack hammer adapted to work on the horizontal. The noise was just as intense, but here in the stope it had nowhere to go. The thing did not so much drill into the rock as it simply rammed into it with sheer brute force, turning the diamond-tipped drill steel a quarter-turn—counter-clockwise, sure enough—between each air pressure-driven surge.

It was a slow, arduous process, but Bob was successfully probing into rock that had lain undisturbed for a billion years. Then he closed the throttle, and the drill abruptly fell silent.

He looked at Jake. "Wanna give it a try?"

"Sure, why not." Jake stepped forward and braced for the weight as Bob relinquished the drill.

It was a struggle just to hold the drill, much less to start or "collar" a hole with any accuracy. Instead, the drill steel skittered harmlessly all over the breast, and Bob quickly intervened, shutting off the throttle.

"You'll never collar a hole that way! You'll write your name all over that breast first!" he yelled. "Here, let me!" He grabbed the drill again and, with amazingly little apparent effort, placed the drill steel tip square in the middle of a painted bull's eye. Then, with a series of short, sharp bursts, he collared the hole.

Each hole took a while. They had to stop to exchange shorter drill steels for longer ones, and even to replace worn diamond bits with fresh ones, and Jake counted twenty-four hole marks in the breast. But once the hole was collared and the drill was hefted into place, Jake learned, drilling deeper was mostly a matter of just holding on, making sure the drill hole was straight and true. If this was "soft" ground, he couldn't imagine the hard stuff.

Once, when Jake had the drill shut down to change steel, the back began to make loud, ominous noises over their heads. It snapped, with a loud cracking sound. Bob just grinned, and waved off Jake's evident alarm.

"Back's just working, is all. Happens all the time. Just remember, when you see *me* runnin' like hell outta the mine, *then* you run like hell."

V

It was a sweaty, exhausting business, but by early afternoon Bob and Jake had finished drilling their final hole and were ready to start loading each hole with Amex, an ammonia-based form of high explosive, relatively inert until set off by some kind of ignition—the igniter cord—which Bob looped in precise order from hole to hole. The trick, Bob explained, was to give each blast, or "shot," somewhere to go, to displace the rock being blasted. If everything went according to plan each eight-foot hole they had just spent the shift so tediously drilling would break cleanly and in proper sequence. Each would displace the surrounding rock into the void just created by the preceding blast. A new heading would then be created, eight feet deeper into the pillar.

VI

Jake wasn't sure he had the energy to make the walk back to the loading station—a mile-and-a-half, Bob had told him—at the end of the shift. But to remain anywhere in this part of the mine when all the blasts were set off—carefully coordinated for the time between shifts when the mine was empty—would mean certain death, so he had no choice but to begin to retrace his steps of the early morning.

At last, to Jake's overwhelming relief, the first bulb leading back to the loading station came into view. Jake couldn't remember ever having been so tired when he and Bob flopped wearily down on the plain wooden benches that lined either wall beside the loading station. Jake noticed his ears were ringing, but he preferred to dwell on how much bonus he and his partner had just earned. They had taken their assigned round, after all. And Bob had even complimented Jake on his promise as a driller. High praise, coming from someone with Bob's experience. Bob was a man of few words, Jake sensed, so even a scattering of encouraging words meant a lot … Yes, he felt pretty good after his first shift—he was no longer a boy now, but a man earning a man's wages. But where was that cage? It began to dawn on Jake, as other men from the level began to drift onto the benches, that he might be in for an indefinite wait. It was rush hour in the mine, after all, and there was but a single cage to lift all the day shift workers to surface …

Jake's mind began to wander to Jo Ann, his girl-friend. Now that he was a bona fide miner, it changed everything. Why, soon he'd be able to buy a car—perhaps even that cherry '57 Chevy Biscayne coupe he'd had his eye on, and they'd no longer need to borrow a vehicle to go and watch the slag pouring.

Watching the slag pouring was the unique local weekend nightly ritual where amorous young couples parked to make out at the base of the sprawling slag heaps in the city's West End, out back of the huge Copper Cliff smelter.

Jo Ann Winters had been Jake's girl all school year, and they were readily acknowledged by their peers as a "steady" couple. Jo Ann might not have been the most beautiful girl in the class and she certainly didn't have the best figure (she was, in fact, rather flat-chested), but she had a ready wit that always made him laugh, and Jake adored the spray of freck-les across her nose and the fair skin of her cheeks. He liked Jo Ann a lot. He couldn't help but think of their last time out parking when the world turned a fiery pink as the molten slag ran like lava after it was tipped from the pots of the hot metal cars high atop the slag heap. The intense heat had inflamed their passion so much that Jake had begun fumbling with the top button of Jo Ann's blouse, —the furthest she'd ever let him go—before she once again told him, politely but firmly, to stop.

Even sitting here on the hard wooden bench Jake felt a stirring in his pants, and, for the first time that day, he caught himself feeling a slight twinge about where he was. As part of his orientation Bob had made him climb one of the wooden ladders that led up out of the mine. It was a precautionary exercise, Bob had explained, because if the power ever failed or the hoist broke down, these ladders would become the only way out of the mine. (And besides, as Bob did not tell his youthful charge, you'd be surprised how many neophytes mastered the back-breaking art of the jackleg and the spooky, scary realm of the stope and the mine generally, only to freeze in terror when it came time to clamber up the exposed, hundred-foot long ladders. That was a deal-breaker in Bob's books.) But, even in his bulky, unfamiliar miner's garb young McCool had climbed slowly but surely to the topmost rung.

Even that one ladder had left Jake feeling out of breath and fatigued, conditions he was at some pain to conceal from Bob. And now, as he thought of Jo Ann's creamy, soft skin and her virginal, forbidden breasts, Jake recalled that one ladder. The thought that some twenty-odd such ladders now separated him from Jo Ann was a sudden, discomforting epiphany. And all that rock between him now and the fresh air, the brilliant light of day! A half-mile of solid rock—all that weight!—suspended overhead! Jake swallowed, shifted edgily on the bench, and told himself to get a grip. Where was that bloody cage?

After what seemed an interminable wait the cage finally arrived. Bob didn't board, announcing he had to attend some kind of briefing with the incoming cross-shift.

Once again Jake found himself in the centre of a tightly packed mass of humanity for the trip to surface.

This time the smell was of sweat, and the mood in the cage was strangely subdued. There was none of the barbed political banter of the morning, which Jake accounted to the fatigue his co-workers seemed to share with him after shift.

But then, after a short interval, the cage's ascent abruptly stopped.

"Young Mr. McCool, I believe this is your stop," said the tender in the same wry tone he'd used that morning as he swung out the heavy steel gate. But now there was a hint of malice in his voice.

Suddenly Jake felt himself being pushed out of the cage, manhandled by his fellow passengers.

"What the f—? What the!" Instantly adrenalized, Jake found himself on some foreign level, one he could sense was unused, deserted, having at some time been removed from production.

But he had more immediate problems, facing a semi-circle of his fellow miners who quickly confronted him with angry, jeering words.

"Well, lookie here!"

"What we got here, boys?"

"What we got here is what happens when a Commie fucks a bitch!"

"Yeah, that's right! Youse get a pinko son-of-a-bitch!"

Wide-eyed in disbelief at this sudden turn of events, Jake was careful to keep his back to the cage door, lest the threatening semi-circle before him become a fully encircling—and probably fatal—ring of pure human hatred.

If only he had a weapon, some kind of equalizer! Jake felt feverishly through the pockets of his coveralls. And there was the crescent wrench Bob had handed him back at the beginning of the shift, which now felt a lifetime ago.

It wasn't much—a standard-issue miner's eight inch crescent wrench—but Jake fished it out and brandished it as he would a knife. And, to Jake's surprise, no one wanted a piece of the hard, rounded end of the thing, diminutive though it was.

The ensuing stand-off gave Jake time to catch his breath and size up his situation. He was badly outnumbered, perhaps twenty to one, and they continued to rain down jeering insults upon him. This explained the quiet in the cage, Jake realized—only one side of the Steel-Mine Mill divide had been represented.

Sticks and stones. Jake continued to slash the wrench through the air in broads strokes, warning off the rush he knew was coming, but no one seemed to want to lead the charge.

Finally, one of his tormentors stepped forward, fists upraised. Henry Hoople. Jake recognized him from the Union Hall as one of the most vocal leaders of the anti-Mine Mill insurgency. An older man with a ponderous beer-gut that strained the zippered front of his miner's overalls, Hoople advanced on Jake, who met him with leveled gaze. Hoople's dark, hate-filled eyes struck him as being too close together. All in all, Jake thought, Hoople's face reminded him of a pig.

He parried the clumsy haymaker right he knew was coming.

Jake's every instinct was to wade right in, both fists flying, but something—some innate sense for self-preservation, perhaps the bone-weariness that lay just beneath the adrenalized veneer of his own aggression—tempered his reaction. Jake sensed that sheer youthful bravado would not carry this day. He dare not advance on Hoople, lest one of the mob edge in behind him.

Instead Jake yielded to his fatigue, his shoulders slumped, and he lowered his guard, turning his back on Hoople, as if in surrender.

"Hey, Harry, will ya look at that! Mrs. McCool's wittle boy wants his mommy!"

Hoople never saw it coming. Jake was certain because as soon as he whirled around he once again locked eyes with Hoople—those stupid, close-set, dark eyes—glittering with malice. Jake launched the blow from the balls of his feet, and only in the instant before it struck Hoople did Jake think he saw a sudden look of comprehension— "Oh!"—just before the eyeballs rolled back in Hoople's head, and he slumped to the deck, dead weight, like a sack of shit, beer gut pendulant.

"Hey!"

"Hey, Harry! You okay?"

Jake watched as the mob rushed forward to attend to their fallen hero. And then, for just the second time that day, he turned his back on them.

And there, like the hand of God itself, was the cage.

2

Big Bill's Young Lad

"You okay, son?"

Jake recognized his inquisitor as Thomas "Tommy" Thompson, the hoist man. Thompson, he knew, was a contemporary of his father's who'd suffered a serious accident underground years before and who had therefore been relegated to light duty on surface— safer, physically less-demanding work, it was true, but also life without the bonus, the mother's milk of a miner's existence. Jake was crossing the shaft house floor when Thompson approached him. The older man spoke in a low voice, which told Jake theirs was intended to be a private conversation.

"Soon's I seen 'em stop at 2150, I figured Hoople and his goons was up to no good. Tender told me what happened soon's he got to surface, so I thought I better get the cage back for ya, just in case."

"Gee thanks, Mr. Thompson. Yeah, it was pretty hairy down there for a while, but we got matters sorted out eventually." Jake rubbed the knuckles of his right hand gingerly. They still ached from the impact of the blow to Hoople's chin.

Thompson shook a head thick with silver-grey hair. "Just wouldn't do, having Big Bill's young lad gettin' hurt, his very first day on the job!"

"Yeah, well, thanks again, Mr. Thompson," Jake edged his way toward the dry. The adrenalin from his confrontation with Hoople had worn off, and all Jake could think of was a long, hot shower to wash away the sweat and rock dust that coated his body.

The dry—how did miners' lingo ever come up with such a name for a shower room? Jake wondered. Typical. A roof was a back, a face a breast, even the drills turned backasswards.

Jake emerged into the early gloaming of a soft May evening a few minutes later, a man transformed. He paused to take stock of his surroundings. Grateful to be back in it once more, he took a deep breath of fresh air, the sweet smell of spring filling his nose and lungs. The earth was just beginning to thaw after the long northern winter, and the air was redolent with a certain mystic, stirring aroma, equal parts rebirth, mystery, fecundity and promise.

It all—all the very best in life—lay before him now, just within his grasp.

There was a hint of a swagger in the step of Big Bill's young lad as he headed for the waiting jitney.

3

Jacob Hamish McCool

"Oh, he did, did he?"

Big Bill was on the phone as Jake entered the back door. The smell of dinner stopped him in his tracks. Meat loaf! He loved his mother's meat loaf.

"Is that so?" Jake's father was on the telephone in his "office," his accustomed spot at the dinner table where he sat each day poring over the Toronto dailies. Big Bill, now retired, was an enthusiastic follower of world affairs, and the morning's newsprint littered the Formica tabletop even now.

"Cold-cocked him, you say? Well, I'll be damned! Well, thanks for the call, brother." Jake stood just inside the door, transfixed by how everything in his parents' house had changed, yet not changed. Big Bill looked up at his son with eyes that were glistening with affection.

Taken aback by this sudden outpouring of paternal pride, Jake hastened toward the living room. All he wanted was to drink a beer, put his feet up, watch TV and relax. But his father intercepted Jake, draping his big hands over his son's shoulders. Big Bill's eyes were moist with pride and affection.

"Good work down there, Son."

Somehow Jake knew he didn't mean the round he and Bob had just blasted.

And then Big Bill did something that he'd never done before: he locked his son in a tight embrace. Jake felt awkward and embarrassed by this sudden bear hug, coming as it did right there in the living room, and in front of the big picture window, a design feature the McCool residence shared in common with every other ticky-tacky bungalow on the street.

The two men stood there for a long minute, a moment Jake would never forget.

"JACOB HAMISH MCCOOL!"

There were few sounds on this earth so fearful to Jake as his mother's voice invoking his rarely spoken middle name.

Jake found her, as he knew he would, in the master bedroom, her arms crossed above her apron, one foot tapping impatiently, smoke practically pouring out of both ears. Jake closed the door behind him.

"What is the meaning of this, young man?"

Jake shrugged, and tried to look innocent. "Nothing. It was just—"

"I don't want you to get involved in this union business!"

"Aw, ma, it was nothing I can't handle—"

"Your very first day on the job!"

"But I had to stand up for—"

"But me no buts, young man!"

"But ma, you should have heard what they said—even about you."

"Pfft! What haven't I already heard! What do you think I didn't hear after I decided to stay with the Auxiliary back in '58 and not go to that rally in the arena?" His mother's dark eyes flashed with pride, anger and determination.

Jake was speechless. He'd always known of his mother's activism in the Mine Mill Ladies' Auxiliary, but he'd no idea that her commitment had been so battle-hardened. Silence descended as they stared defiantly at each other, and the awareness sank in that they had fought—were fighting—for the same thing. Good Lord, thought Jake, I get this from both sides of my family. He *is* a scrapper, thought Alice McCool. Just like his father at that age.

The silence lingered as mother and son appraised each other anew.

4

Jacob in the Whale

Even though he was retired and no longer strictly speaking a member in good standing of Local 598 of the International Union of Mine, Mill and Smelter Workers, Big Bill still attended the monthly members' meetings of the big Local, imperiled as it now was by a sinister insurgency of mysterious but powerful and well-organized origin. The elder McCool was like an old boxer answering the bell. And on this early spring evening Jake decided to tag along. Not that he cared about one union over another, but what the hell?

The big Union Hall was packed, the air charged with tension and cigarette smoke so thick you could cut it with a knife. Big Bill drifted off, melting into the multitude, leaving Jake to survey the scene. And it was quite a scene.

A single, wide aisle ran down the centre of the big room, splitting the rank and file right down the middle. Jake spotted Henry Hoople on the right hand side, and, judging by the glare Hoople shot his way, Hoople also spotted Jake. Hoping to stay out of trouble and remain inconspicuous, Jake quickly found an empty chair in the rear, on the left hand side. Even those last few empty seats were filling up around him.

At the front of the big hall a half-dozen or so men in suits and ties—the Local Executive—sat behind a row of tables high up on the elevated stage. They looked down on the roiling mass assembling below. In between them stood a single, imposing, mustachi-oed man behind a wooden lectern, resplendent in a three-piece suit and tie. This was, Jake knew, Spike Sworski, president of the big Local.

Sworski rapped the podium with his gavel, calling the meeting to order. The hub-bub on the floor fell to a low, angry buzz, and Jake's attention began to wander ...

His eyes were drawn upward to the expansive, vaulted ceiling of the great room—one of the largest indoor spaces in the city. The whole affair was sup-ported by a series of beefy wooden beams that soared upward out of the wooden floor that always reminded Jake of a gym floor, the beams arching up and then curving, angled, to join overhead at the centre of the ceiling.

Laminated wooden beams, as beautiful in their soaring, upward curve, at least to Jake's eyes, as any-thing in any church ... Wooden because, as Jake's dad and uncles had recounted to him a million times, the Mine Mill Hall had been built in the aftermath of the Second World War, when steel was still in short supply. The inherent self-reliance and resourcefulness of sev-eral thousand determined hard rock miners had devised this solution to the architectural conundrum, trumping the co-efficients of load bearing over daunting distance and height by interlayering and interlacing hundreds of two-by-sixes.

The rows of soaring beams always reminded Jake of giant ribs. He felt as Jonah must have felt, in the belly of the whale.

"Mister Chairman, Mister Chairman!" An angry, stentorian voice interrupted Jake's daydream. Hoople was on his feet. "Point of Order! In light of the clear and present danger represented by godless world Communism to our free and democratic way of life, Mister Chairman, I propose that each and every member of our Executive Board should be required to immediately swear an Oath of Loyalty to the Queen, and to the government of the Dominion of Canada, and to further swear that he is not now, and has never been, a member of the Communist Party of Canada!"

Hoople's dark hair was shiny with sweat from all that yelling. It *was* stifling in the Hall, Jake realized, and Hoople's angry oration seemed to turn the temperature up a few more notches, as his backers leaped to their feet, bellowing their support, and the members on Jake's side—including, he supposed, his father and uncles, they must be up in front there somewhere—jumped to their feet and roared back across the aisle. Sworski banged his gavel furiously. "Order! Order! The brother there is recognized!"

A rank-and-filer on Jake's side remained standing as those around him simmered down and sat down.

"Mister Chairman, Local 656 of the United Fishermens' and Allied Foodworkers' Union is now in its second month on strike out in Vancouver, and I move, Mister Chair, that this Local Union donate one thousand dollars to the Fishermens' cause, as a show of solidarity in their courageous stand against the rapacious greed of the fish plant owners of this country's West Coast!"

"Whaaat?" The right hand side of the room erupted in a great roar of calumny.

"There ya go! Another Commie outfit!"

"Why should we—"

"Order! Order!" Sworski, who towered over the rank and file on the floor, was banging his gavel furiously once again. "There is a motion on the floor!" Even though it was amplified over the public address system, Sworski's voice was barely audible over the din. "Do we have a seconder?"

Someone on Jake's side quickly raised his hand.

Sworski carried on, unperturbed by the howls of outrage from his left. "It has been moved and seconded that we donate one thousand dollars to the strike fund of Local 656 of the United Fishermens' Union, to support their heroic struggle. All those in favour?"

A forest of upraised arms surrounded Jake.

"All opposed?"

The mass across the aisle signalled its unified opposition.

"The motion is carried!"

A howl of outrage greeted Sworski's words, forcefully echoed by triumphant cheers from those around Jake.

Sworski continued to hammer away with his gavel, to little avail.

"Point of Order!" Hoople was on his feet again, so irate that a single lock of black hair now hung down over a forehead glistening with sweat. One of his shirttails had worked its way loose over his paunchy belly.

"Point of Order, Brother Chairman! Aw, fuck you! Challenge the Chair, Mister Chairman! I challenge the Chair!" Hundreds of burly miners around him bellowed their leather-lunged support of Hoople.

Sworski shook his head emphatically, calling repeatedly for order, except that now the uproar had become so boisterous that his actions carried back to Jake only in pantomime.

And so Jake never did really hear Sworski's declaration that the unruly meeting was adjourned.

Only the shuffling of feet and scraping of chair legs on the hollow-sounding hardwood floor told Jake that yet another disastrous membership meeting of Local 598 had drawn to a close. As the members began to drift back out toward the entrance the jeering continued. It was a wonder to Jake that no one came to blows as the two factions funneled shoulder-to-shoulder through the exits.

At length, Big Bill located his son in the crush. He draped a paw over his son's shoulder.

"So, whaddaya think? Comin' out for a few beers with your uncles?"

Jake readily agreed. It was early yet, thanks to the meeting's abrupt end.

After all, it was thirsty work, running the largest Local Union in all of Canada.

5

The McCools Ride Again

Two generations of McCools adjourned to the Nickel City Hotel. Just a few blocks down the hill from the Mine Mill Hall, the Nickel City was a favourite watering hole of Mine Mill loyalists.

Jake found himself at a small circular table, the top of which was covered with clear glasses brimming with draft beer. Beside his father and his two brothers, they had been joined by Spike Sworski himself, much to Jake's surprise. The union leader wasn't drinking much beer, Jake noticed, but he joined right in on the stories the elder McCools were sharing about the rough-and-tumble days of organizing the union.

The warm memories and laughter were flowing as freely as the beer when Jake first noticed them, a half-dozen Borgia hard cases, headed straight for the table, almost at a run, their faces hard-set with malevolent intent. The wrath of God.

And then the bar erupted with the racket of breaking glass and overturning tables. His father and uncles were on their feet even before Jake, whose attention was riveted by one of the invaders who was headed straight for him. No! He was after Sworski! As he squared to confront him Jake noticed a dull glint from the attacker's right hand. Knucks! The son-of-a-bitch was wearing brass knuckles! When the guy led with his right, Jake side-stepped the blow, grabbed his wrist, and yanked hard enough to pull him off balance. Taking no chances against such potentially lethal force, Jake stood above his attacker and stomped down hard—twice—on the arm holding the knucks.

Then, and only then, did Jake think of his dad. Big Bill was on the other side of the table, his back to his brothers. The elder McCools had formed a tight circle, each of them brandishing a jagged shard of a broken draft glass, daring anyone to come near. No one did.

Evidently the interlopers had seen enough. Almost as quickly as they had converged on the McCools they vanished, out the door and into the night.

Everyone at the table was hyperventilating, rearranging his clothes and laughing slightly in relief. Sworski tugged down on the vest he was still wearing beneath his suit coat. Jake wasn't sure how many punches he'd thrown.

"I hardly know how to thank you, young man." Sworski extended his hand to Jake.

"Jake McCool. It's an honour, Mr. Sworski."

"Ah yes. Big Bill's young lad. I've heard of you." Then Sworski stepped back and surveyed Jake and his elders with a sardonic grin. "The McCools ride again, I see."

And then, to Jake: "Why don't you come see me at the Hall next week?"

6

Into the Night

They rode silently at first, father and son, up well-lit Notre Dame Avenue, through the Flour Mill, the city's venerable French working class district, just north of the downtown core.

But after they crossed Lasalle Boulevard and headed deeper into the Valley the streetlights became scarce and the enveloping darkness lent the car's interior a sense of intimacy. Jake at last broke the long silence.

"So is he?"

"Is who what?"

"Is Sworski a Commie, like they say?"

"Son, I honestly don't know. What I do know is he's a good union man, honest and true to the rank and file."

Jake was well acquainted with the familiar dichotomy—in Sudbury you were either "a union man" or "a company man." There was no middle ground.

"But the '58 strike, dad, you can't tell me that wasn't a fuck-up."

"No, I can't. But remember every member gets a vote in this union, and the members voted to go out. Spike was just following the will of the membership."

"And so what if some of 'em are Commies?" Big Bill pressed on. "It's a free country, and we don't ask a man what his party preference is before he becomes a member of the Mine Mill ... Despite all the persecution we've faced down in the States our union has done some great things. Did you know, for example, that down in the Deep South we long ago admitted Negroes as full members and even leaders right alongside our white members?"

Jake didn't. But he knew his father was referring to the growing unrest in the deep southern states like Alabama and Mississippi where lunch counter sit-ins and bus boycotts were all the rage as young protesters of both races were beginning to deploy non-violent tactics against the deeply rooted segregationist policies of the Jim Crow South.

"Sworski took the lead when your Uncle Walt and Uncle Bud and I pitched in to organize the union back in the Forties, that's all I know. I couldn't prove he *is* a Commie, couldn't prove he isn't ... Besides, what if some of 'em are Commies, like they say? They've still provided some mighty good leadership to this union over the years. They built this union. And what else really matters?"

They had crossed over the rocky, treeless height of land that separated Sudbury from the Valley they were dropping down into, a series of scattered, sprawling subdivisions where the McCools had taken up residence just a few years earlier in Farmdale

Subdivision in Hanmer. Jake paused in the conversation to take in the lights of the Valley as they glittered, stretching off for miles to the north on the Valley floor. Jake never tired of the sight.

"He wants to meet with me next week," Jake told his father as they pulled into the driveway.

"Spike?"

Jake nodded.

"Does he now?" Big Bill yanked on the parking brake. "Hmmm … Maybe better not tell your mother about that. Or what just happened at the bar."

Jake nodded again.

7

Crossing the Rubicon

"Mr. Sworski will see you now."

Jake had been cooling his heels in the inner sanctum of the Mine Mill Hall, studying the heretofore off-limits upstairs office area with keen interest.

He was shown to a seat by a crisply efficient secretary, who then returned to her desk behind a glass partition. She wore a telephone headset and pounded away at her typewriter when she wasn't answering the telephone, which rang incessantly. Occasionally a man in a suit—Jake recognized each of them as members of the Local Union Executive who'd been sitting up on the stage at the membership meeting—would emerge and exchange a few words with the secretary before disappearing again into a row of offices down a hallway.

Finally Sworski himself came down the hallway, and, after greeting Jake cordially, invited him into his office.

The space itself was nothing special—small, rather spartan quarters with a window overlooking Regent

Street and Queen's Athletic Field, a big wooden desk, a high-backed desk chair, a few cardboard boxes, evidently containing old files, stacked in a corner—Jake took the chair facing the desk, and studied Sworski, who was now ensconced in his office chair, which tilted, pivoted and rolled around on casters. As a result, Sworski was never still. He was in his forties, Jake guessed, precocious for a position of such power. With his neatly trimmed moustache, gnatty three-piece suits and gentle manners, the ever-dapper Sworski had a courtly, old country air about him.

"So," Sworski began. "The reason I've asked you to come here today. What happened at the bar the other night," he paused with a rueful smile, "I'm afraid it's but a sign of things to come. The Steelworkers will not rest until they've smashed this Local Union and, quite possibly, me along with it."

Jake listened in silence.

"I've seen you in action, young man. Your reputation precedes you. You're from a good Mine Mill family. I'd like you to become my personal assistant, to accompany me in, ah, shall we say situations of some difficulty, and there will be many such situations in the months to come, I fear."

Slowly it dawned on Jake: Sworski was asking him to become his bodyguard!

"Oh, I don't know, Mr. Sworski, my mother would never— "

Sworski cut him off with the wave of a hand.

"I spoke with your mother just now. Everyone remembers Alice McCool and what she's done for this Local Union. While you're right, she certainly wasn't crazy about the idea at first, she did come around to the idea it could afford you an opportunity, besides the, ah, risk."

Jake, impressed, sat back in his chair.

Sworski pressed on. "We would, of course, work around your regular shifts and, in the event of scheduling conflicts, arrange with the company for an excused absence on the basis that you're attending to union business, which, in a manner of speaking, you would be …

"The, ah, position will be remunerated on top of your Inco pay, of course. The amount must first be approved by the treasurer, and I'm afraid it will not be overlarge, especially considering the demands on your time and the, ah, danger that may well be involved."

Jake tried to take it all in. The thought of earning more money, over and above his Inco wages and bonus, certainly appealed. Rather than being intimidated, he was attracted to the prospect of scrapping for a living—or part of one, anyway. And he quite liked the idea of spending more time with Spike Sworski. For reasons he couldn't quite put his fingers on, he found himself liking the man very much. Certainly he'd never been around anyone quite like the union president.

Sworski looked at Jake across the big desk. "So, we have a deal then?"

Jake stood up, and stretched out his hand. "Yes sir, Mr. Sworski. We have a deal."

Sworski chuckled and shook Jake's hand. "Splendid. Splendid. I look forward to it."

Jake was surprised at the softness of Sworski's hand, so unlike his father's, Bob's, or even his mother's.

Still in a daze, Jake excused himself from Sworski's office before swiftly descending the stairs leading from the union offices.

There are moments and there are moments and then there are moments in all our lives that are, if we but knew it, mini-Rubicons. Such was the moment in the life of Jake McCool as he paused on the curb to await a break in the traffic streaming past on Regent Street in front of the Mine Mill Hall that steamy June evening in 1963.

Some things—the unmistakeable whiff of sulphur that begins first as an acid taste in the back of the throat—Jake senses.

Others—the ancient Siren song of danger, adventure, wealth and beautiful women that has lured young men since the time of Odysseus—are also clear enough to Jake as he waits for the river of chrome to part that night.

But the more profound and subtle portents pass him by, as they nearly always do in such moments. He does not sense the air currents stirred by the wings of the year's first returning Monarch as it floated over Queen's Athletic Field. He does not hear the preternatural death rattle of the leaves in the scrub poplars studding the lip of the basin that ringed the running track surrounding the field—an odd sound for so early in the summer—as the foliage burned beneath the dirty yellowish cloud that was even then descending over the intersection of Regent and Elm Streets.

Instead Jake, finding his opening, bites back the aftertaste of sulphur, swallows and plunges headlong off the sidewalk, into Regent Street and into history.

Mine Mill Local 598 Hall (Oryst Sawchuk)

PART TWO

To Catch a Killer

8

Is Bob Dylan a Communist?

It was early yet and his parents weren't expecting their car back until later, so Jake headed straight for Jo Ann's to tell her his exciting news.

"Oh yes, Jake. She's right here. Won't you come in?" Jo Ann's mother appraised him coolly at the front door, her eyes red-rimmed and swollen. Neither of Jo Ann's parents cared much for Jake, high school drop-out and semi-rounder that he was, and not from a particularly promising family, either. A *Mine Mill* family.

Mrs. Winters ushered Jake into the living room where he found Jo Ann playing records. As always, Jake was impressed with the Winters' home—the scale of it—the rooms were so much larger than his parents' place. And the smell of it—every room, it seemed, was infused with the aroma of cigar smoke— so much richer and more exotic than the smell of Export A and Sweet Caporal cigarette tobacco that his own dad and mom smoked. And then there was the stereo, nested in the top of a long wooden console that also contained the Winters' television, as well as a pair of stereophonic speakers. Their stereo played the latest, newest thing in high fidelity recorded music—long-playing, vinyl records that turned at 33-and-a-third revolutions per minute, while the McCools were still stuck with the much-heavier, much-scratchier old 78s. No way his parents, who still insisted on paying cash for everything, would ever waltz into the store and plunk down a thousand bucks for such a thing. They maintained that any form of debt—"buying on time," as they called it—was nothing more than a bosses' plot to ensnare the unwary working man. Jake was just resolving that with his first paycheck he'd head straight for Eaton's to buy his own hi-fi when Jo Ann approached him with a record cover in her hand.

"Oh, Jake, I'm so glad you've come! You've got to hear this new album I just got in the mail today from the record club!" She handed him the record cover. He glanced at it and saw a photo of a skinny young guy he didn't recognize walking down a wintry city street with a pretty girl on his arm. They both looked cold.

"Has your mom been crying?"

"Yes, the sulphur came in and burned her garden just now. Killed her plants and all her flowers just like that!" Jo Ann snapped her fingers for emphasis.

"Oh. That's too bad." Jake found it impossible to feign much interest in flower gardens. That was one advantage of living in the Valley: inconvenient as the longer drive into town often was, at least they were out of range of the worst of the smelter fumes.

"This just came out." Jo Ann pointed at the skinny guy with big hair and cowboy boots striding through the snow with his hands jammed into the pockets of his blue jeans. "Bob Dylan. You've heard of him?"

Jake shrugged. Not really.

"He's the one who wrote 'Blowin' in the Wind.'"

"Oh, sure." Who hadn't heard that? The anti-war ballad sung by the folk trio Peter, Paul and Mary was played incessantly on both CKSO and CHNO.

Jo Ann turned back to the stereo, let the needle drop, and Jake heard "JO ANN WINTERS, NO! NOT THAT HORRIBLE THING AGAIN! MUST WE? THAT YOUNG MAN CAN'T CARRY A TUNE IN A BUCKET!" as Mrs. Winters objected loudly from the kitchen.

Even here, in a house so much more spacious than his own, privacy was impossible, Jake realized.

Jo Ann sighed loudly.

"Very well, Mother! I'll take Jake up to my room, if that's okay—"

It was, as both Jake and Jo's mother understood, more a statement than a question.

Jo Ann snatched the album cover out of Jake's hands, scooped the record off the turntable and led Jake by the hand to the plushly carpeted stairs.

Her room always struck Jake as a foreign country, filled with stuffed toys, adorned with pink chiffon. And, most importantly on this day, her very own portable hi fi. It had a hinged lid and removable speakers on wires that could be moved around the room for the best stereophonic effect. Jo Ann let the needle drop again and they both listened in silence as "Blowin' in the Wind" filled the room. But in this version the pretty vocal harmonies of Peter, Paul and Mary were absent, replaced only by a strummed acoustic guitar and a single gravelly male voice that seemed to channel an oracular, timeless wisdom. Jo Ann's mother was right about one thing: this guy really couldn't sing.

"Jo Ann, I've just come from the Union Hall, and—"

"Shhh! Shush Jake! Listen to this!"

Jake lapsed into obedient silence and was drawn into music unlike any recorded music he'd ever heard—spare, unadorned tunes rasped out by that raucous voice accompanied only by a strummed six-string guitar, and the occasional harmonica break, an off-key screech that sounded like the alley cats of early morn. But what really sucked you in were the words. Brash, angry, accusatory, the raspy, howled lyrics fused the anger of youth—a resentment that Jake, Jo Ann and just about everyone their age shared—at the cloying beliefs their parents held so dear—in material things, in religion, in the Cold War, in institutions like *unions*—with melodies that were flat and compressed, and yet appealing …

". . . so we can buy a car even sooner." Jake concluded his news when the music finished at the end of the record.

Jo Ann frowned. "Wanna hear the other side?"

"Sure." And it was true. He *did* want to hear what came next.

And once again they fell silent, swept up in a world where youth dared to question everything; a world turned upside down.

"I dunno, sweetie, it sounds dangerous." Jo Ann bit her lower lip, as she always did when something worried her.

Her dark brown eyes, which at other times could beam with mischief and wonder, were clouded now with worry and self-doubt as she crossed the room to face him.

"Jake, do you think Bob Dylan is a Communist?"

"*What?* I dunno. Why do you think that?"

"Well, he's obviously against war, and they say he went down into the South, to sing to the Negroes, and now you're going to work for Mine Mill, and even Mr. Sworski personally, and just last Sunday Father Legault preached about the need to be constantly on the look-out for Communists. They're everywhere, apparently. Especially around the Mine Mill Hall."

"Oh Jesus, baby! Not you, too! Look, I'm around the Mine Mill Hall because Spike Sworski offered me a job, that's all. We can use the money. I can buy a car, and then, who knows? Maybe I can even get a place of my own! Here! Let me check!" Jake lay out flat on the floor before lifting the pink chiffon bed skirt under Jo Ann's bed. "Nope, no Commies under the bed. I checked."

He could see she was not amused.

"Aw, c'mon, Jo. Just because someone supports civil rights and speaks out against nuclear war doesn't make 'em a Communist! Look at what happened last year over Cuba! We just can't keep doing this! 'Masters of War,' he's right! We'll blow ourselves right off the face of the earth if we're not careful."

But Jo Ann's frown remained, and Jake paused, drawing a deep breath. What a time they were in! She was still chewing on her lower lip. The chafing made her lips even pinker, and swollen.

Finally, Jake drew her to him, into his arms, and did what he'd been aching to do the entire afternoon: he began gnawing hungrily on that lower lip.

9

Brother in Arms

Jake barely recognized him—Ben had changed that much in just one short school year. And yet there was no doubting that the scruffy, guitar-toting stranger who stood looking up at him in the "Arrivals" area now was indeed his brother Ben.

"Hey there, little brother."

"Welcome home, big brother."

Jake held his older brother at arm's length, looking him up and down.

"You-you've changed." It was true. Ben's hair was longer than he'd ever seen it, and it looked as if he hadn't shaved in days—weeks, even.

"What's Mom gonna say?" Jake was dubious.

Ben laughed, waving aside Jake's reservations. "Not to mention the old man, eh? Well, let's go find out."

"Don't you have any luggage?"

Ben pointed down at the soft-sided guitar case resting on the airport floor. "Naw, just underwear and a toothbrush, is all. It's all in there. Let's go face the music."

For as long as Jake could remember, he and Ben had always shared a bedroom, so it was only natural that he'd stay in Jake's room on the spare bed now, during this summer's visit.

They'd just sat down on their beds when Jake eyed the guitar case.

"Can you actually play that thing?"

"A little. Wanna hear?" Ben reached down and unzipped the case.

"Sure."

Ben lovingly pulled out an old Gibson, and began tuning, before picking a melody, which Jake recognized as Bob Dylan's "Don't Think Twice, It's All Right." The second time through, Ben even sang along.

Jake sat in dumbfounded silence. So much had changed since the fall, when Ben, also a talented enough hockey player, had left home to attend college at the University of Michigan on a full-ride athletic scholarship. Such things were non-existent in Canada, and Bill and Alice were hard-pressed to decline the chance for their middle son to gain a free college education at a first-rate university, even though it was in a different country. The decision had actually been easier for Alice, who, strictly in private, harboured special affections for her middle son. Ben was different from his father and brothers. His comparatively diminutive stature lent him a sense of vulnerability that the taller, raw-boned McCool men lacked. Ben was her dreamer, with his nose in a book often as not. This gritty old mining camp, with its beer-and-hockey macho culture, was no place for a boy with Ben's spirit and sensitivity. And she dreaded the prospect that he might end up in the mines, with their lure of fast money and the ever-present spectre of sudden death God knew how many ways. So many miners were killed each year it barely made the papers. No, far better to ship her middle son off to a brighter, if uncertain, future out of this sulphur-blasted God-forsaken place.

The sight of their scruffy, guitar-toting son, though, had given both Bill and Alice pause.

Jake, however, was intrigued by the change. Although he was smaller, Ben was two years older, and so would always be Jake's "big" brother. And, even though he was six inches shorter, Jake had always looked up to the brother who sat across from him now. He'd never been much of a reader, but it was Ben who had introduced Jake to *Catcher in the Rye*, when Jake was still in junior high. Jake had devoured the book, finding a kindred spirit in the outlaw worldview of Holden Caulfield.

"So-so how is it down there?" Jake asked finally, after the last strains of the Dylan tune had faded away.

Ben shrugged. "Oh, the hockey season was so-so. But what was really interesting was what happened off the ice ... Ever hear of the SDS?"

Jake shook his head.

"SDS—that stands for the Students for a Democratic Society. I ended up joining the Ann Arbor Chapter."

"But I thought you were down there to play hockey."

"Sure, but I'm still a student, and some grad students from my political philosophy class invited me to a meeting, so I went."

"So what do they believe in, this SDS?"

"The biggest thing is participatory democracy, I guess."

Ben noticed his brother's vacant stare.

"Participatory democracy. People should have control over the decisions that directly affect their lives, is all ... And the other thing that really got to me was that at the meeting they were all talking about something they called 'white skin privilege.'"

"Were they black?"

"No. And that's just the thing. None of them were black, but they were very concerned about black people ... I never thought of it that way, you know? That we have some kind of privilege just because we were born with white skin."

Jake shrugged. "No, me neither. But it does make sense, kind of."

"It was the first time I'd ever been around people who were more concerned with others, rather than with just their own futures. And that made me think."

Jake reflected in silence on his brother's words. He felt almost embarrassed at Ben's new-found conviction. It was almost as if Ben had suddenly decided to convert to some new, seemingly alien, religion. He studied his older brother as he began noodling absentmindedly on the well-travelled, mellow sounding Gibson. He was attired in a blue workshirt, with the sleeves rolled up and blue jeans over scuffed brown leather cowboy boots.

Suddenly Jake brightened, and sat up straight.

"Hey! Wanna go into town and hear some live music? Jackie Washington's at the Coulson."

This time it was Ben who returned a blank stare.

"Jackie Washington! Great old blues man from Hamilton!" Jake was already heading for the door.

"Sit tight. I'll see if there's enough gas in my car ..."

Coulson Hotel, Downtown Sudbury (Oryst Sawchuk)

10

Participatory Thuggery

Well, it was certainly the same old Coulson, Ben thought to himself as he surveyed the crowded, noisy bar. Same old reek of cigarette smoke and stale beer and piss that always seemed to overpower the deodorant placed in the urinals in the men's john.

Same old crowd, too. Rough downtown trade, staggering unsteadily from table to table in search of the next romance, the next high, the next free beer. Raggedy ass—bad teeth, bad skin, unhealthy—the unmistakable air of poverty, the underbelly of any mining camp, lambent just over the brassy veneer of the noise, colour, motion and music. At least that was cool. Jake was right about this cat Washington. A black bluesman with an infectious smile, Jackie was of an indeterminant age, and his hundred-watt grin and sly, salacious groove lit up the room.

Ain't no use in me workin' so hard
Got me a gal in the rich folks' yard
Kills me a chicken

Sends me the wing …
Thinks I'm workin'
Ain't doin' a goddamned thing …
… But I'm thinkin' bout her—
Her, and a dozen other women …

It struck Ben as the kind of place where someone could get stabbed any minute. Toto, we're not in college any more.

Jake scooped his draft glass off the table and began to wander through the big room, just checking out the action. He spotted Paul Dunn leaning against the far wall. An aspiring blues man in his own right, Dunn was intently studying Washington's licks, grinning broadly at the lyrics of the performer's talking blues. Paul spotted Jake and nodded. Jake nodded back, lifting his glass in mute salutation.

They stayed until closing time, and then drifted out into Durham Street with everyone else. The crowd had thinned out as Jake and Ben turned up the laneway beside the Coulson block. They were alone when he came at them from the shadows of a doorway. Jake instinctively squared up to fend off the dark-clad assailant whose face he couldn't see in the dark alleyway. But to Jake's surprise their attacker took a step back, turning sideways and lashing out with a kick that struck Jake in the kneecap. It felt like his knee had exploded. Jake hit the asphalt, hard, and he was still flat on his back, watching helplessly, when the guy went to work on Ben with the pipe. His brother did what he could to defend himself, but Ben was no match for the much larger attacker, who was working now with cool, murderous efficiency. The only sounds were of metal on bone, Ben's moans, Jake's howls of outrage and the grunts of their assailant as he put the boots to the now-prostrate and defenceless Ben. Jake himself felt faint at the suddenness and lethality of it all. Eventually, though, there was one other sound as their attacker, his work evidently done, stood over them, breathing heavily.

"There, you little Commie motherfuck. Participate *that!*" The pipe made a hollow metallic clang as he threw it down on the pavement of the alley.

And then he was gone.

The events that followed were a terrible blur. Jake finally gathered himself enough to roll over and check on Ben, who was already going into convulsions, his legs and eyelids twitching. He didn't respond either as Jake shook him, screaming his name into the dark night. Finally Jake composed himself enough to hobble back out onto Durham Street, where he beseeched the last of the Coulson crowd to call for help.

Jake hurried back to Ben, and cradled his brother's head in his lap. Ben was no longer convulsing, but he was still unconscious, with frothy bubbles of something—Jake couldn't tell in the dark, but he hoped it wasn't blood—forming on his lips, and then the police arrived, a pair of detectives in shapeless, ill-fitting suits, skinny ties, both wearing fedoras. The dicks were next to useless, all but yawning and scratching their asses as they plied Jake with questions about yet another back-alley mugging of lowlifes at Coulson closing time. They hadn't either the sensitivity or the suppleness to even crouch beside Jake as he sat on the greasy asphalt attempting to comfort his brother. Instead they loomed overhead and spoke down to him. No, they weren't robbed and no, he hadn't seen their assailant's face well enough to make an ID. He had no idea what had provoked the attack. Yeah, he would meet them back at the cop shop later to make a full statement. The ambulance attendants arrived next. They searched for a pulse in Ben's neck, found none and pronounced Ben McCool, his head still in Jake's lap, dead at the scene. Ben was twenty-one.

Next they turned their attention to Jake who was beginning to shiver in the steamy night air. They bundled him into a woolly blanket, helped him onto the stretcher, loaded him into the back of the ambulance where there was, at last, just enough light to allow Jake to see clearly that his long, waking nightmare had just begun.

11

Burden to Bear

The funeral was held at Christ the King, a venerable, dark-brown bastion of Catholicism overlooking downtown Sudbury. Jake was surprised to see Spike Sworski among the mourners. He hadn't seen the union leader since the night of Ben's murder. This bum knee was really putting a crimp in his income. The thought shamed him immediately. Here Ben wasn't even in the ground, and Jake was thinking money.

Jake was even more surprised when the priest yielded his pulpit to Sworski. He was his usual dapper self in a three-piece summer-weight suit with a matching pocket puff and tie. Sworski's gaze swept over the crowded church, and then lingered over the McCool clan, sitting shoulder to shoulder in the front pew.

He nodded slightly at them and cleared his throat before extracting a pair of reading glasses from his vest pocket. "I know Ben McCool was not formally a member of our union," he began. "But in his honour, and in honour of his family, I think it only fitting that I read the following from the Mine Mill Union Burial Service Ritual. These words, I believe, date back to the Western Federation of Miners, the union of legendary leaders like Big Bill Haywood and Joe Hill. They were the first to organize hard rock miners in western North America, fighting successfully for the eight-hour day and many other amenities and rights we now take for granted. The Western Fed was formed in 1893, and was the predecessor union to the International Union of Mine, Mill and Smelter Workers."

Sworski paused, and then began to read from his notes:

"We are now to pay our last tribute of friendship and brotherly love to one of our members who has laid down the burdens and responsibilities of life."

Alice McCool dabbed at her eyes.

"No more will his voice be heard in our councils; no more will he feel the gentle touch of love for kindred and friends, or tender pity for the unfortunate and afflicted, for his heart has ceased to beat; no more will he experience the beauties of nature or experience the joy, the pleasures or the sorrows and distress of this life. He sleeps his last long sleep in the grave. We yet have a burden to bear; we can yet find enjoyment in this life; but to him these have passed forever. He has gone to 'that land from whose bourne no traveller e'er returns.'

"Will his eyes open on a better and happier land, a land where there will be no sorrow and no weeping, but a place of eternal happiness? Our reason says perhaps, while the hope and loving of our hearts says yes. And now, as we deposit the sprig of evergreen and consign the remains of our brother to their last resting place let each one resolve 'to so live, that when thy time comes to join that innumerable caravan, which movest to that mysterious realm where each shall take his chamber in the silent hall of death, thou go not like the quarry slave at night, scourged to his dungeon; but soothed and sustained by an unfaltering trust. Approach thy grave like one who wraps the drapery of his couch about him, and lie down to pleasant dreams.'

"Goodbye, Benjamin."

Jake's mom was weeping silently but openly now, as Sworski descended from the pulpit and gently laid a cedar tip on top of Ben's closed casket.

Jake was surprised how moved he felt at the union leader's words and demeanour, which lent so much dignity to the service. But then, he had never heard the man speak in public when he wasn't being heckled, hounded, badgered and otherwise vilified.

Sworski then stepped to the front pew where he paused to console each of the McCools in turn, bending slightly to shake hands with each of the men, and to whisper a few words.

"I'm truly sorry about your brother, Jake ... Come see me at the Hall next week. There's someone I'd like you to meet."

Jake nodded.

12

Gilpin

Jake sat in his accustomed chair in the anteroom on the second floor of the Hall. Or at least he started to, before rising to his feet and beginning to pace the floor. He'd found it nearly impossible to sit still since the night of Ben's murder. Whenever he was alone and idle lately, like when he was trying to fall asleep, all the torments and self-doubts returned. The truth was, he blamed himself for Ben's death; how could he not? It had been his idea, after all, that they go into town to that ratty old Coulson.

Sworski's approach interrupted Jake's torrent of self-recrimination.

Jake expected to once again be ushered in to the president's office, but instead he was led down an unfamiliar hallway and shown into a large room filled by a long table. A single man sat at the table, a pen and notebook in front of him.

"Jake McCool, Foley Gilpin," Sworski began. Jake shook hands with Gilpin who, he thought, might just have been the ugliest man he'd ever seen. His head seemed too large for his body. And it was shaved bald—or nearly so. It was fringed with a short, fuzzy growth that served mainly to call attention to Gilpin's egg-shaped head. The man struck Jake as a true egghead.

"Foley's a newspaperman—and an old friend— from Chicago," Sworski hastened to add, perhaps sensing Jake's immediate ambivalence about Gilpin. "He's come up to help us fight off the Steelworkers." The trio sat down at the boardroom table.

"Now, Jake, we just have a few questions about what happened that night—that night with Ben …"

It was Gilpin who led the way, questioning Jake closely about that terrible night. The newsman recorded Jake's answers meticulously in his notebook. Here, at last, was the kind of debrief Jake had expected from the police. Finally Jake reached the point where the pipe clattered to the ground.

"And you're quite sure that's exactly what he said? 'Participate *that*, you little Commie motherfuck?'" Gilpin frowned at the words.

"I'm sure, yes sir."

"What do you think he meant by that?"

"I-I'm not sure. But just before that Ben had been telling me about this new club, or something, at his university that he'd joined, Students for Democracy or something, and how they believed in participatory democracy as a way to make things better … I've wondered ever since if there was some connection …"

Gilpin nodded. "Yes, Students for a Democratic Society. I've heard of them … And you say he turned sideways and took a step backwards instead of attacking you head on? And then he lashed out with a kick?"

Jake nodded, and Gilpin's frown deepened. The newspaperman took a deep breath, shook his head, and then threw his pen down onto his notebook. The interview was over. Sworski stood up. "Well Jake, thanks for coming in today." Jake took his leave of Gilpin, and Sworski walked him back down the hall.

Sworski returned to the boardroom immediately, and sat down next to Gilpin. "Well Foley, what do you make of this?"

The newsman grimaced, and shook his head. "Nothing good I'm afraid."

"Why?"

"Start with the way they were attacked. Clearly this was no run-of-the-mill mugger if young McCool's description is accurate. The assailant fought like someone specially trained in hand-to-hand combat. That tells me he's ex-military. Former Airborne, maybe. They're trained to kill like this, by hand, using stealth, and at close quarters. So are the Green Berets, Marine Corps, Rangers, the SAS in England. These are elite outfits, their members are few and far between, and to be here, in the streets of Sudbury?

"It makes no sense, unless ..."

"Unless?"

"Unless the Agency has started to take a special interest in the raiding of your union."

"The Agency? You can't mean the CIA! Interfering in the affairs of a friendly nation? Surely even they wouldn't dare!"

"Don't kid yourself, Spike. They've been operating behind the doctrine of plausible deniability for at least the past ten years. They'll cover their tracks so well that no one will ever be able to prove they were even here—not you, not anyone else. Not now. Not ever."

Sworski listened in silent, stubborn disbelief, but Gilpin noticed that the colour was beginning to drain from his friend's face.

"And that means you have a problem, my friend. You're up against not only the Steelworkers' Union, but also an outfit with the resources of the U.S. government … I don't put it past them to run a covert operation right here, right under our nose—after all, they overthrew the Arbenz government in Guatemala back in '54 … Popular, democratically elected government out on its ear. They used the local press to discredit him, the Catholic clergy got into the act, and Bob's-your-uncle the world's once again safe for the United Fruit Company."

"But, but how did you learn this, if it was all so clandestine as you say?"

Gilpin answered with a shrug and rueful grin. "Because I was there. Paper sent me down to cover it. Turns out Chicago has an inordinate number of shareholders in United Fruit, along with the Dulles boys. You've heard of them. Brother Allan ran the CIA and big brother John Foster runs the Sta—"

Sworski cut him off with an impatient wave of his hand. "Yes, yes I know who they are."

"The government of Jacobo Arbenz Gutman was elected with a mandate to implement land reform—to take land from the huge landowners, like United Fruit, and distribute it to poor, landless peasants, many of them Maya Indians. But this threatened the profits and dividends of United Fruit, and was construed as Communist influence in the region. A paramilitary force was trained and equipped by the CIA, they invaded and, combined with a robust black ops campaign that included setting up a special radio station with a powerful signal beamed straight into Guatemala—the Voice of Liberation, don't you know—Arbenz was gone in a matter of weeks. Soviet influence in Uncle Sam's backyard was ended, and the Monroe Doctrine was restored. No outside powers allowed into the Western Hemisphere, which still includes Canada, last time I checked. And not only that, didn't you tell me the brothers Dulles are on the board of the big company here, International Nickel?"

Sworski could only nod glumly. There was no doubt about it—he was definitely looking pale.

Gilpin let out a short, sarcastic laugh. "Not the kind of fellas to sit idly by and watch a 'Commie outfit' like Mine Mill gain a chokehold at the company that produces eighty to ninety percent of the free world's nickel, *their* company, after all. Without nickel as a steel alloy there'd be no B-52s, no Bomarc missiles, no nuclear warheads."

"Yes, yes, I know all that," Sworski agreed impatiently. "But even if what you're saying is true and they went so far as to send an assassin up here, why target Benjamin McCool? Why not his brother, who was my bodyguard, after all? That I could understand, at least. That would make some sense."

Gilpin pondered for a moment, and shrugged. "Maybe that would have seemed too obvious. The trick here is to get in and get out without arousing suspicion ... Plausible deniability. This way they deal a body blow to one of your foremost families, send a message, without raising undue alarm among the local authorities. My guess is they're not done yet ... They'll drag a red herring across the trail to divert all attention away from the murder of Ben McCool ..."

"Jesus Christ," was all Sworski could say. He was now as pale and shaken as if he had just glimpsed a ghost in broad daylight. Which in a sense, Gilpin reckoned, he just had.

13

To Catch a Killer (I)

When it came, the summons reached Jake through his mother, who was tapping gently on the bedroom door and whispering his name.

"Jake? Jake, there's a phone call for you."

He rolled over, still caught up in his dreams and in the tangled sheets, which felt clammy, as they often seemed to be these days.

Jake clawed his way up into wakefulness, and out of bed. He sat for a minute on the edge of the bed, running his hands through bed-tousled hair. Then he slouched to the door, and, clad in his socks, skivvies and T-shirt, padded out to the dinner table where his father sat, surrounded by a sea of newsprint, his arm extending the telephone.

Jake cleared his throat as he reached for the handset.

"Yes?"

"Jake, it's Foley Gilpin here. Met you at the Mine Mill Hall."

"Oh! Sure, I remember you, Mr. Gilpin."

"Listen, I have a proposition for you. I'm in need of someone to help me out—drive me around, show me the sights—someone who knows the lay of the land. Spike says I can 'borrow' you, and that the union would pay you for your time, at the going rate. Interested?"

"Sure!" Jake didn't hesitate. He was heartily sick of spending all day loafing at his folks' house. Besides, he was broke. Even though he no longer needed his cane, the doctors still wouldn't approve his return underground.

An hour later they were together in the Chevy and Jake was pondering where to begin with Gilpin. He decided to give him the truly big picture. "No one really knows for sure, Mr. Gilpin, but the geologists are starting to think that the Sudbury ore body— and the Sudbury Basin itself—were created when a giant asteroid struck the earth right here, and then skittered across the earth, gouging out the Sudbury Basin before it went skipping off back into outer space.

"This was billions of years ago, mind you, so there was no one around to see it, but the collision was quite a thing. Scientists believe it was more powerful than all the bombs ever exploded in every war in recorded human history, including Hiroshima and Nagasaki. The impact was so powerful that it cracked the earth right open, right down to the core, and the Sudbury ore body was formed when molten streams of the minerals from the earth's core bubbled up into those cracks. So that's where the minerals came from."

Jake paused to see if the newspaperman was following, but a quick glance at Gilpin's studious expression convinced Jake that he was.

"Okay, so the Sudbury ore body is what's known as a massive sulphide deposit, which means that the valuable minerals are widely distributed in minute quantities throughout much larger blocks of rock of no value—what we call 'country' or 'host' rock, as opposed to ore, or muck. It's so finely distributed, in fact, that we often have to displace a ton of rock just to get an ounce or two of nickel!"

"Really!" The visitor was clearly impressed at this fact, as Jake had hoped he would be. "And yet you can still make a profit by extracting an ounce per ton?"

Jake nodded. "But that's just about the lowest grade that's still profitable, and that's the fine line between worthless rock and valuable ore, you see. Less than that—it's just rock. More than that—say an ounce or two per ton—and then you're talking high-grade ore, and we're in business. Of course a lot depends on what happens to the ore once it's hoisted, and that's what I'm going to show you now—the mills, smelter and refineries that purify the raw muck into pure metal, nickel and copper, and even silver and gold, here on the surface. Ready?"

His guest nodded, so next Jake started on a tour of the production cycle, showing Gilpin a few head-frames, explaining how whole small company towns—Garson, Creighton, Levack—had sprung up around the mines in the outlying areas. The company owned everything out there, Jake told Gilpin: all the houses, town councils, even entire police forces. Then he took Gilpin to the smelter at the heart of that mother of all company towns, Copper Cliff, just west of Sudbury, and finally to the Copper Cliff refineries where finished nickel, copper, gold and silver were produced.

Then Jake showed Gilpin the neighbourhoods of central Sudbury—the Flour Mill, West End, Gatchell, Minnow Lake, the Donovan, Little Britain and the Borgia, that central, decaying agglomeration of flophouses, brothels, fleabag hotels and tenements. Already talk was starting that the entire district should be razed and replaced with some form of urban renewal.

Gilpin had seemed particularly impressed by the westernmost residential neighbourhoods, the Gatchell and West End, where the slag piles loomed over the tidy stucco bungalows, forming a flat, black horizon so vast that no end could be seen. Gilpin directed Jake to drive here and there before he hopped out of the car to take pictures. He had visited West Virginia coal towns where the slag dumps towered over everything, but they were nothing like this—the sheer immensity of Sudbury's smelter slag piles, their surreal height and expanse, forming a jet black, stark contrast with the neat green yards and the lovingly tended backyard vineyards of the heavily Italian residential neighbourhoods. Sudbury was a visually striking place, there was no doubt about that. A picture was still worth a thousand words, and so Foley Gilpin, a born wordsmith, fussed endlessly with his picture-taking, ever striving for just the right exposure, the perfect angle. Finally, he climbed back into the car.

Jake found the Chicagoan a quick study—his questions pertinent and to the point. Which prompted a question from Jake. They were sitting outside the Copper Refinery building, at the end of Jake's "nickel tour."

"So tell me, Mr. Gilpin, what are you really doing here?"

"Well, as Spike told you, I'm here to help out with the raids—write radio ad copy, press releases, that sort of thing. But right now I'm trying to get to the bottom of what happened to you and your brother Ben. I have a theory ..."

Jake listened intently.

"But so what if we do catch the guy? What happens then?"

Gilpin sighed. "You're right. Chances are they've already exfiltrated him, and he's long gone by now. But Spike's given me some time off my regular writing duties to see what I can turn up ..."

Even with Gilpin's disclaimer, Jake was excited despite himself.

"Whatever I can do to help, Mr. Gilpin, you just say the word."

After all, what harm could it possibly do to spend a few hours trying to catch a killer?

14

Rivers of Fire

They parted ways just before suppertime—Jake to arrange a last-minute rendezvous with Jo Ann, Gilpin to continue with his discreet inquiries, a probe he hoped would arouse no local interest or suspicion.

Jake managed to catch Jo Ann just before her family dinner, which she gladly ditched in favour of grabbing a burger with Jake.

He found her wearing cutoffs and sitting barefoot on the front lawn, her long, bare legs drawn up before her, chin resting on her knees, enjoying being out of the cloying family atmosphere on this evening in the fading summer. Just the sight of her made Jake ache with happiness and longing. He could almost feel the grass between her toes as she ambled to the curb to meet him, sandals dangling from her hand.

"Where we goin', Sparky?"

"Deluxe?"

"Sure," she assented happily, as she climbed into the passenger seat.

Within minutes they were seated on the hard plastic seats of a booth at Deluxe Hamburgers, the city's newly opened, locally owned burger chain, celebrated—in Sudbury, at least—for the tastiness of its milk shakes and French fries. Both of them had ordered the cheeseburger basket—easy on the onions—with a vanilla shake.

Foley Gilpin, meanwhile, was off to his own solitary, pre-arranged rendezvous with a cub reporter from the city's only newspaper, in pursuit of his own personal Holy Grail—proof that the CIA was indeed destabilizing an otherwise peaceful community in a country that was a close neighbour, friend and ally of the United States. What a scoop that would be; Pulitzer material, almost surely.

Gilpin and the rookie, who was assigned to the police beat on an interim basis, adjourned to a nearby bar. The youngster was eager to talk shop with a veteran from a big-city American daily. Long practiced in the art of eliciting information without revealing any, Gilpin also learned that:

- No murders had been reported that summer.
- The kid's newspaper was probably the most hated daily in its market that Gilpin had ever encountered, owing to its long-standing anti-union bias in a strongly pro-union market (the paper's influence was waning even as the union's influence was growing as Mine Mill aggressively moved to organize unions among local musicians, waiters and barmen).

- As a result of its unpopularity the local paper perpetually struggled to maintain its circulation, and, thus, ad lineage.

The hours passed swiftly, and by the time Gilpin and the kid emerged from the bar it was growing dark. Out on the edge of town Jake and Jo Ann had parked at the base of the sprawling slag heaps, waiting for the pouring of the slag to start. It was a little like waiting for it to grow dark enough for the drive-in movie to begin. Jo Ann slid across the front seat to sit beside Jake, who put his arm around her. They sat that way for hours as the colour drained from the sky. Jo Ann's bare leg was right next to Jake, and eventually he mustered the courage to place his hand atop her thigh. He was tantalized by the short, dark hairs he could see there, soft as down to the touch. She said nothing. Finally, at dusk, an electric locomotive appeared at the top of the black slag, high above them.

"Let's get out and watch," Jake suggested.

They clambered out of the Chevy and climbed up on the front bumper. Soon they were sitting on the hood, which was still cooling down from the heat of the motor.

The warmth of the metal was welcome in the cooling evening air.

It wasn't much of a train. There were only two cars behind the loco. It was twilight now—difficult to see what was happening atop the slag heap—and for the longest time nothing much was. Sound replaced sight. There was the eerie, mysterious banshee wail of metal on metal, made still spookier by the cool descending dark that was falling now all around them. They both shivered at the imminence of what lay ahead.

Finally the trainmen tripped the slag pots, and rivers of fire began to stream down the embankment of the slag pile. The molten slag was almost too bright—and too hot—to look at directly. The intensity of the heat was alarming, and more than a little frightening. Eventually the train was shunted back and forth and back and forth before the second slag pot was tipped. Now more rivers of fire ran down parallel to the first, which was already cooling down to a dull glow.

Jake and Jo Ann returned to the car, Jo Ann once again cuddling into Jake's arm. The top of her thigh was warm to his touch now, warmed by the rivers of fire. But the insides were still cool and goosebumpy as he began to stroke her there with smooth, gentle motions. Soon the friction of his hand had warmed her skin, and the goose bumps were gone. Gradually he brought his hand higher and higher up her thigh, until it touched the fraying fabric of her cut-off jeans. He began to kiss her, and she opened her lips to his, shuddering beneath his touch. He put his fingers, languidly at first, inside her cutoffs, testing her reaction. To his amazement and eternal gratitude, she seemed only to increase the intensity of their kiss. Next he began to probe with his fingers, feeling the down between her legs, the moist warmth there, and now he was well and truly aroused and he felt the pressure welling up inside, welling and swelling, and sensation was running from his fingers to his groin like an electric current, like a private, intimate river of fire between them. She felt it, too, he could tell, by the way she was moving, arching her hips to welcome his greedy, questing fingertips. His arousal was white-hot now, undeniable, and he felt as God must have felt at the instant of Creation, and his heart was in his throat, and he was filled to bursting and instinctively he was about to move on top of her and ... the dam did burst and he buried his head in her lap and he was crying, in great, gasping sobs that shook his shoulders, and she was cradling his head in her lap, stroking his hair, cooing his name, not missing a beat, her initial surprise transformed seamlessly to soothing, as she said his name over and over, "Oh Jake, oh Jake, it's all right, baby, everything's going to be all right." But the realization that nothing would ever again be all right, that this, this moment in the dashboard light beneath the swiftly cooling slag, that she was all he had, the only person in the world that truly understood him, made his sorrow more tender still, deepening his inconsolable, gasping sobs, and he buried his face even deeper in her, clinging to her with all the desperation of a wounded, cornered animal.

Downtown Foley Gilpin turned toward the westering sky and the apocalyptic, brilliant pink light bursting there. Anywhere else he might have felt alarmed— surely half the city must be on fire. But Gilpin was oriented now, knew which way was west, and so saw the slag pouring for what it was—the slag was being poured, that was all.

15

The President Hotel Caper

Jake picked Gilpin up the next morning as if nothing unusual had happened the night before.

The newsman, still lugging his camera bag and attired in his usual rumpled suit, asked Jake to drive him to the Union Hall where he left Jake waiting in the now-familiar antechamber while Gilpin went in for a private meeting with Spike Sworski.

Fifteen minutes later they were back in the car.

"Do you know where the President Hotel is?"

"Sure." Everyone knew the President, one of the city's foremost downtown hotels, a straight shot downhill on Elm Street, past the courthouse and jail, across Lorne, and soon they were pulling into the parking lot behind the President.

"Follow me," Gilpin instructed.

They entered the back entrance and rode the elevator to the sixth floor, where they faced a long hallway lined on either side by hotel room doors. Gilpin tapped his forefinger to his lips in the universal signal to remain silent. Then he led the way down the hall, evidently searching for a particular room. When he found it, Gilpin backed up against the wall, leaving Jake, feeling fairly ridiculous, to do the same on the other side of the door.

They stood that way in silence for a moment, listening. Jake could just make out a voice through the door. It wasn't much, but it made his skin prickle, and the hair on the back of his neck stand on end. Jake's eyes widened in disbelief, a reaction that was not lost on Gilpin.

"That's him!" he mouthed at Gilpin. Gilpin nodded, pantomimed to Jake that he wanted him to break the door in, and then everything happened very fast.

Jake kicked the door in, wood splintering as the dead bolt and door jamb gave way, and Jake was rushing into the room headlong, Gilpin right behind, and then Jake stood straight up and began backing right out the door, almost tripping over Gilpin.

As he rushed in Jake saw two men on the single beds in the room. One was tall, angular, his razor cut blonde hair rising to a flat-top crewcut. He was reclining comfortably on the bed, a cigarette dangling from his lips, awaiting a light from the outstretched hand of the second man in the room who was—Stanley Winters! The shock of recognition hit Jake as surely as if a powerful hand had pushed him squarely in the chest, knocking him backward so swiftly that he almost fell over Gilpin.

Before Gilpin knew what was happening Jake was pelting back down the hallway, toward the elevator.

They both retreated to Jake's car, Gilpin's camera gear bouncing around his belly as he ran. They arrived breathless and nearly hysterical from surprise, adrenalin, and confusion.

Gilpin caught his breath first. "What the fuck was *that*?"

Jake had a death grip on the steering wheel of his car despite the fact that the ignition was still turned off. "That—that was my girlfriend's father. And what the fuck was he even doing there, with the guy who killed my brother? And what were *we* doing there?"

Gilpin nodded and swallowed, hard. "Tip from Spike. He's got some guys selling Steelworker cards ..."

This information drew a quizzical look from Jake, as Gilpin had expected.

"That way they're trusted, in a good position to get information ... and it seems the Steelworkers have reserved that room more or less permanently for when their out-of-town staff organizer's in town to run the raids, which is most of the time these days ..."

Jake, who had caught his breath now, was nodding. "And it led us straight to our killer ..."

"Yeah, and what does that tell ya?" Gilpin asked Jake.

Jake, who was still processing the morning's revelations, shook his head in dumbfounded silence.

"So, where to now?" he asked Gilpin.

"Fucked if I know."

"Yeah, me neither."

16

The $64,000 Question

In the end, Gilpin decided, he wanted to go back to his room at the Caswell. The cross-town trip afforded the duo a chance to gather their wits.

"So what does he do?" Gilpin asked Jake, as he steered them through the maze of Killer's Crossing.

"You mean my father-in-l—?" Jake caught himself. "His name's Stanley Winters. I don't know, really. He's some sort of bigwig at the company ... But what I don't get is what he was doing *there*? And with *him*? And in a room paid for by the *Steelworkers*?"

"Yes," Gilpin nodded somberly. "That *is* the $64,000 question."

Jake drove around aimlessly after he dropped Gilpin off. Normally he would have headed straight for Jo Ann's, to share the latest news; a clear impossibility now, for so many reasons.

That realization, coupled with the morning's events, made Jake feel lost, as if he had slipped his moorings. With a heavy heart he pointed the Chevy north finally, toward the Valley.

17

Gilpin Muses

For his part, Foley Gilpin adjourned directly to the lounge at the Caswell, a quiet, dimly lit refuge presided over by a crisp bartender who was a proud, card-carrying member of Mine Mill Local 902—the new Local that 598 had spun off to represent their newly organized food and beverage worker members. The bartender had become a prime source of information about a city that teemed with intrigue, rumour and paranoia.

How did that old saying go? Just because you're paranoid doesn't mean they're not out to get you. Gilpin slid onto his favourite stool at the bar and ordered a beer. He needed to think. First and foremost, he had found his killer. And sure enough, with that buzzcut the guy had ex-military written all over him.

They had seen their man, true, but he had also seen them. Would he act to silence them? He would have recognized young McCool, almost certainly, but probably not Gilpin himself. Did that mean his young friend was in danger? Gilpin doubted that. Audacious as he was, the mystery killer was unlikely to touch Jake. Two murders in a single family inside of two months would be impossible to ignore, even for this city's semi-somnolent police force.

So, where did all this leave him? Did he have enough for a story? His gut told him yes, his head something else. First, connect the dots. He had no doubt they'd found their man, especially given Jake's reaction at the hotel. Gilpin considered young McCool to be highly credible. Gilpin's earlier hypothesis—that the CIA was in cahoots with the Steelworkers somehow—now also seemed highly plausible. Equally plausible was the likelihood the Agency would deny, deny, deny any involvement in fomenting Cold War hostilities—much less committing murder—in a Canadian city most Americans had never heard of. Hell, even his own editor couldn't find Sudbury on a map. Gilpin's heart sank at the very thought of Wally Rasmussen, that mountain of flesh who inhabited, Buddha-like, the slot at Chicago's largest circulation daily. Even now Wally would be scowling imperturbably in the slot, surrounded by phalanxes of hovering copy clerks and wire editors attending to a cacophony of ringing telephones and the ceaseless tinkling of alarm bells on the hulking wire service teletype machines.

And here Gilpin's brain took over. It was no secret in the newsroom that he—Gilpin—was the butt of open jokes from Wally and Hildebrand "Hildy" Norman Thayer III, the paper's Washington bureau chief, senior White House correspondent and star reporter. Wally fairly worshipped Hildy, whose stories ran page one above the fold, as often as not. Whether they deserved such play Gilpin often wondered. But there was no doubting Hildy's pedigree—elite Eastern prep schools, Harvard man, tall, handsome and rich—which lent him considerable cachet around the Kennedy White House. He was also a frequent invitee to the chi-chi Georgetown dinner parties favoured by so many of the Kennedy insiders. Both Hildy and Wally made little attempt to disguise their contempt for Gilpin's personal crusade to expose the Central Intelligence Agency and all its works. They considered Gilpin's dogged, lonely, investigative efforts to be a quixotic quest at best, paranoid lunacy at worst.

So no, in other words, he probably had no chance of getting what he now knew into print.

Gilpin sighed, and ordered another beer. And what did he really know?

Foley Gilpin could barely suppress a smile at the thought of what was likely happening now—the phone lines to and from Langley were probably already burning up as the mystery man reported that morning's events. He was made—his cover blown—he'd have to tell his handler. And what of that handler? Why had he left his asset in place after Ben McCool's murder, risking exposure of the mission, and of the Agency's role in the Sudbury raids?

As part of his ongoing investigations Gilpin had made it a point to debrief retiring Agency personnel who would never have dared to speak to him while they were still on active duty. Gilpin had learned that Langley-based handlers often had many assets in the field at once and that, while no one wanted to actually admit it, some were known to lose track of, or even, on rare occasions, to simply forget about one of the agents under their control. If the asset was operating behind the Iron Curtain the result of such neglect, however momentary, could mean his exposure, capture, interrogation and execution. In a friendly theatre like Canada, as events were showing, such dire consequences were far less likely. Which might have increased the likelihood that Langley had indeed forgotten about the stone-cold killer it had dispatched to Sudbury, Gilpin mused. If so, he could imagine the derelict handler scrambling even now to find the most expeditious route to Sudbury to assume first-hand charge of damage control over any fall-out stemming from his and Jake's sudden visit to the President Hotel that morning.

And what to make of the presence of Jake's girlfriend's father with the killer in a suite paid for by the Steelworkers? Jake said the guy was some sort of bigwig with International Nickel, which certainly gave the lie to the company's official line that it was strictly neutral in the Steelworkers-Mine Mill dispute. So what *was* he doing there?

Gilpin suspected he was a cut-out, a local go-between at the centre of the CIA-Steelworker-Inco axis. Certainly there was something in his servile demeanour toward the killer to suggest they knew one another—and fairly well. Still, in the end, Foley Gilpin realized with another sigh, all he really had were more unanswered questions.

Gilpin drained his beer and headed for his room.

18

Two Disappearances

Jo Ann and her mother were used to the prolonged absence of the family patriarch, so neither of them gave much thought at first to Stanley Winters' failure to return home at the end of August.

Neither Jo Ann nor her mother knew exactly what he did at Inco; balding, bespectacled and bowlegged in a mousey kind of way, Stanley Winters worked long hours at Inco's Ontario Division office in Copper Cliff when he was not flying to Toronto for hush-hush meetings with the top corporate brass at Inco's Canadian headquarters in a high rise office tower high above Bay Street. Whatever he did, Stanley Winters was certainly an excellent provider—his wife and only child were ensconced in a spacious, handsome home in the city's most exclusive and desirable residential district.

Jo Ann was, truth be told, much more worried by Jake's absence than she was her father's. Why, Jake hadn't even called since their last date, that passionate, somewhat bizarre encounter at the slag pouring when poor Jake had ended up bawling like a baby with his head in her lap. Her father, both Jo Ann and her mother assumed, had gone off on yet another business trip. But Jake's silence was not like him. He was always calling or dropping over, eager to share the latest news in his life.

Jo Ann's mother took the call that would change their lives forever. It came on the Wednesday before the Labour Day weekend, and Jo Ann was able to overhear the conversation clearly.

"Yes?" her mother said into the telephone.

"Speaking."

"Yes, it is."

"No, I'm afraid he's not home right now."

"I'm not sure ... Gone to Toronto on business, I'd imagine ... Why? Is something wrong? No! That's impossible!" Jo Ann looked at her mother, who suddenly turned white as a sheet and sank into a kitchen chair. "Are you sure it was Stanley?"

"Mother, what is it?"

"It's your father. That was the police. They say he was just hit by a bus downtown. He's gone, Jo Ann."

"What? Gone where? You don't mean—"

"Yes, he's dead."

They collapsed into one another's arms, weeping in great moaning sobs.

Nothing that day was destined to go as Jake expected as he joined the steady stream of black-clad mourners entering the funeral home. He was so nervous about seeing Jo Ann again that he'd almost talked himself out of attending the wake about a hundred times that Labour Day weekend. But she saw him first. Jake never did even make it to the large reception room upstairs at Jackson and Bernard where Stanley Winters' closed coffin was on prominent display. Instead Jo Ann was in a smaller anteroom, reserved for smokers, packed with younger mourners, many of whom Jake recognized from school. Jo Ann rushed up to Jake as soon as she spotted him loping uncertainly toward the reception room.

"You came!" she blurted in evident surprise, as she stopped just short of Jake, looking up at him, those familiar green eyes scanning his with dozens of mute questions. Jake knew the questions, but not the answers. He touched her on the elbow, and steered her gently away from the crowd.

"I-I'm sorry about your dad, Jo."

"Oh Jake, what happened? You stopped coming over, you didn't even call—"

"I know, I know … I'm sorry, Jo …" he trailed off, helpless in the face of the truth, which was the one thing he couldn't speak, especially now.

"What happened, anyways?"

Jo Ann shook her head, fighting back the tears. "Oh, the police say it was an accident—nobody's fault, really. They say Daddy was crossing against the light and he wasn't in the crosswalk … You know how absentminded he could be …"

Jake nodded solemnly at her explanation before pulling her softly into his arms, his mind racing, incredulous at the news that Stanley Winters had stepped right out in front of a bus in broad daylight in downtown Sudbury, in the middle of a sunny summer morning.

PART THREE

In the Upper Country

19

A Skating Rink in Hell

In any sort of global, circumferential sense, Sudbury's miners had barely scratched the earth's crust as they drilled and blasted their way into the Sudbury ore body. But three successive generations of hardrock miners had, in their pursuit of the rich Sudbury ores, probed relentlessly to still greater depths, leading them ever closer to the molten centre of the earth. While they remained thousands of miles above the raging, red-hot magma that filled the earth's core, Sudbury's miners had, by the 1960s, begun to encounter the heat that radiated from that core.

The heat was intense enough, as it dissipated from the molten core through solid rock, to present another discomforting challenge to the workers who toiled in the drifts, headings and raises that honeycombed the earth beneath Sudbury's streets like some giant ant farm.

Of course, the problems were more severe in some places than others.

As a general rule, the deeper the mine, the hotter the conditions. The heat at Creighton #9 Shaft, the Basin's—and the Hemisphere's—deepest mine, at 9,000 feet, was legendary.

It was not a problem Jake—cleared by his doctor to return to work in mid-September—had expected to encounter at Frood Mine, a relatively shallow operation, but that first morning in the cage he couldn't help but overhear a conversation about the heat in the mine's bottom country, at a mere 2,400 feet.

"Muck's so hot you can't pick it up, *tabernouche*, a hundred degrees, she burn you good, misterman."

"Yesterday me and my partner had to wet the breast, cool it down, before we could even load our rounds," affirmed another voice in the darkened, gently rocking cage.

"No wonder it caught fire down there," observed yet another anonymous voice.

"Burn, baby burn," laughed a gruff voice, just as Jake arrived at his level.

He was discharged at the 600 foot level, Frood's "Upper Country."

He found Bob Jesperson waiting at the loading station. Aware they had combined to form one of Garson's most productive teams—not to mention highest bonus earners—management had decided to keep the duo together and to assign them to the high grade stopes of Frood Mine's Upper Country.

Once again, Jesperson led the way down the drift to their stope. It was a short walk. As they surveyed their new workplace Jake noticed how chilly it was.

"Headings up here all break into the pit," was Bob's explanation.

It took a minute for Jake to understand. Like most hard rock mines in Canada's Cambrian Shield country, Frood Mine had begun its life as an open pit operation. But, after ever-increasing depth had rendered the method impracticable, the mine's owners had at last opted to sink a shaft into the ore body, to begin the more expensive process of underground—as opposed to open pit—mining. At Frood that shaft was immediately adjacent to the vast, deep—very deep—hole in the ground left by the pit.

What Bob was saying was that the levels they were extending would eventually break through the wall of the pit. As a result the ambient temperatures in the pit were felt in the stopes, as they were this frosty September morning.

"Jesus Christ!" Jake responded at last. "You mean to tell me we're working in an ore body that's on fire and we're freezing our nuts off?"

Bob laughed heartily at Jake's consternation. "No grass growin' on you, chum. Fire's down at 2400, been going for years, you hardly ever smell it up here. But the cold's no joke. Works into the heading, ground freezes in the winter, thaws in the summer, expands and contracts, loosens things up somethin' fierce. Just about as bad ground conditions as I've seen in all my years in the Sudbury camp." Bob shone his cap lamp toward the screened off back. "Look't that loose! It's hangin' up there like a bunch a' grapes! You think you're cold now, wait'll December! What we got here is a skating rink in hell, Jake. Fire down below, freezing up above. Welcome to Frood Mine. Well, pitter-patter, let's get at 'er."

And with that Bob hefted the jackleg into place, hit the air, and collared the hole.

20

Jake Banks the Bonus

With its myriad of levels, drifts and headings a modern hard rock mine is a vast place, with hundreds of workers dispersed through many miles of vertical and lateral space. The very nature of this three-dimensional maze makes it a difficult place to supervise, an activity made even more challenging by hardrock miners' storied self-reliance and fierce independence. In every mine there lingered accounts, however apocryphal, of an especially mendacious shift boss being literally run off a level by a pair of exasperated, wrench-wielding partners whose patience with supervision had long since worn dangerously thin. The fact is, most hard rock miners work unsupervised most of the time.

How then, to ensure that they toil to maximum effect, maintaining both productivity and profitability, to continue the flow of dividends to far-off shareholders in Toronto, New York City and London?

The time-honoured solution: incentivize the miners' labour through a scheme known as the individual mine production bonus. While it seems simple (the individual is remunerated on a rate based upon the cubic measure of the muck displaced during a given pay period) the bonus system, as Bob now began to teach Jake, is, in fact, highly complex and dense with nuance.

It was lucrative, yes (bonus earnings are commonly expressed as a percentage of hourly pay; a highly successful bonus miner earns "one hundred percent bonus" or double his already lucrative hourly wage).

But the system also has severe downsides, Bob cautioned Jake. It rewards cutting corners because the metric is based strictly on tonnage—whether that muck is produced safely or not had no place in the equation. And, to the degree that working safely (properly screening the back, for example, or not drilling bootlegs) does not itself enhance production, human nature dictates that an ambitious bonus miner will too often maximize the time spent on hardcore production at the expense of safety-related matters like rockbolting and screening. Frontline supervisors were measured first and foremost by tonnage: did the headings under their purview meet pre-set quotas? The raft of serious injuries that left the lucky merely maimed for the rest of their lives, and the unlucky dead, were an unfortunate concomitant of the hardrock mining industry. "After all, Mr. Coroner, a mine is not a chocolate factory," the company's pinstripe-clad lawyers were fond of reminding the coroner's juries summoned to study the circumstances surrounding yet another miner's death, now a monthly occurrence in the Sudbury camp.

But the conceit that accidents happened only to the other guy was a fool's game, Bob warned Jake, especially here in the Upper Country, with its truly terrible ground conditions.

Another troublesome aspect of the bonus system, Bob, ever the shop steward, observed, was that it fell entirely outside the collective bargaining agreement between the union and the company. Unlike virtually every other aspect of the miner's life on the job, the bonus system was not negotiated. Oh, there was a "contract" all right, in that a production team leader would "bid" on a particular heading after carefully weighing factors like ground conditions, probable tonnage and likely bonus rates. But which crew was assigned which stope was ultimately the prerogative of management. This, too, invited arbitrariness and even favouritism on the part of management, which, in turn invited the boatloads of grievances that were duly filed about work assignments.

But even those commonplace and long-running disputes were trivial compared to the visceral matter of the bonus rates. Here again the company had the men by the short and curlies, for the rates were a slippery, contentious matter under the exclusive control of the company. Suppose he and Jake consistently made one hundred and ten percent bonus, Bob would rant, waving his sandwich for emphasis as they ate their lunch on the muck pile. Then sure as shit some white hat with a clipboard would show up, right here in the stope, to study their every move. These so-called time-motion experts would measure every distance, time every move, and within a week, wouldn't you know it, their bonus would fall to ninety percent even though they were pulling just as much muck as before. "New bonus rates" would be the company's only explanation. And what the hell? It was true he and Jake had no say over, or even any idea about, how the bonus rates were set. If this *was* a chocolate factory it'd be called a good old-fashioned speed up, having to work twice as hard, to avoid a twenty percent cut in pay.

It went without saying that he and Jake, like bonus miners everywhere, had long since come to consider the bonus an essential part of their paycheck, absolutely necessary to support themselves and their families. Every penny would be spoken for before the cheque had even been cashed, every penny necessary to maintain the lifestyle to which every miner, and his wife and children, had become accustomed. Even single guys like Jake burned through the money like there was no tomorrow. Shiny new muscle cars (GTOs, Sting Rays, Dodge Chargers), four-wheel drive trucks, bigger and better gadgets (colour television was the latest, next best coming thing), boats and motors, expensive new stereos, there was no end of must-haves in Sudbury's fast-paced, boom-town lifestyle.

Simply keeping a roof over one's head was also an increasingly expensive challenge in a city acutely sensitive to events half a world away. As the United States ramped up its war in Vietnam, demand for nickel, "the most militarily strategic of metals," soared, and with it both the world nickel price and the profits of the International Nickel Company, all of which reverberated with Jake and Bob, their ears still ringing from the roar of the jackleg, as they ate a hasty lunch in the dark, dusty confines of their stope on the 600 foot level of Frood Mine on an afternoon in early October of 1963.

Job seekers from all over the world were flooding into the Nickel City, hoping to share in the fast money, and the city was bursting at the seams. Venal home owners rented every spare room and space to the newcomers, to further augment already rich wage and bonus earnings. The practice of "hot sheeting"— where a bed, cot or couch was rented to both a day-shift worker and his cross-shift counterpart—was not uncommon. One newly arrived immigrant family found themselves forced to dwell behind the basement furnace of an already-established Sudbury family, so great was the housing shortage triggered by the nickel boom of the 1960s.

"But there's a few things we can do to beat the system," Bob confided, lowering his voice to a conspiratorial tone. "One is slowing down when them time-motion assholes are down here with their clipboards."

"Working slower?" frowned Jake. "But that'll mean less bonus, for sure."

"For that one shift, sure. But it's how they'll set the rates for months to come, which'll let us earn as much as before, don't you see?"

"The second thing we can do is to bank the bonus."

"Bank it how?" Jake looked up with interest.

"We under report our breakage for most of a pay period, so it looks like we're not making so much bonus. And then, at the end of two weeks, we draw down the bank, report our actual breakage, and we're back to a hundred percent, or even more."

"I get it," Jake nodded, chewing his sandwich thoughtfully. "They think we're making less than we actually are, so they don't come down to cut our rates. But really, we'll still be making a hundred percent."

"You got it, Pontiac."

"Let's do it, then." Jake stood up, gulping down the last of his lunch with a swig of now lukewarm coffee. "Pitter-patter ..."

And so, on that afternoon and for the rest of the pay period, Jake and Bob began to bank the bonus.

At first, it all went according to plan, with no inkling that the scheme could be fatally flawed.

They shaved just enough off their reported daily tonnage, or "push," to reduce their bonus nominally, but not enough to arouse the suspicion of management.

Meanwhile in actuality, of course, they continued to make their steady push at their accustomed one hundred percent rate, perhaps even more. It was a grind, but in the meantime Jake continued to learn the nuances of successful, safe, high bonus-earning hard rock mining from Bob, techniques that would serve him well for the rest of his life: how you had to work smart, and not simply bull-bull, to be a big-time bonus miner—learning to think ahead before crossing the heading, for example—and to anticipate whether you should carry this or that tool with you now, to save steps later. Time was money, after all.

Safety was another major challenge here in the Upper Country. Jake learned the delicate, life-saving art of scaling by watching Bob. Each day they'd begin their shift by cautiously venturing into their heading, which had just been blasted by their cross-shift. They were entering a space, still dusty from the blast, created only minutes before in rock that had lain undisturbed since the earth cooled. All eyes were on the back. On a good day most of the screen would still be intact. Bob would venture as far out under the edge of the screen as he safely could, being careful not to advance beyond the screen, which basketed any loose that might have scaled off the back. He'd grab his scaling bar—a heavy, six-foot-long bar made of solid cast iron, blunt at one end, tapered at the other—and begin tapping on the back. A ringing sound was reassuring, Bob explained. The ground was solid. But a dull, spongy, sound was a sure sign of loose, no matter how solid the ground might look in the dull beam of their cap lamps. Here Bob would search for an opening, insert the tapered end of his scaling bar, and begin prying and prizing at the suspect ground in the back, and often, sure enough, a chunk of loose would come crashing down to the floor of the stope in a shower of rock dust and splintering fragments. Sometimes, it might be the size of a basketball, but at others it would be ugly, fearsome chunks weighing untold tons and leaving no doubt as to its lethality. "Falls of ground," as they were termed by Ministry of Natural Resource statisticians, were among the leading, if not *the* leading, causes of death among hard rock miners in the province.

The greatest precaution—and this too was only relative; every man who stepped onto the cage knew the risk he was facing by venturing underground—was to always work only beneath the screen, which was laboriously advanced by drilling and bolting into the back. The drilling was done with a device known as a stoper, basically a jackleg adapted to drill vertically. Instead of filling the freshly drilled hole with Amex, a rockbolt, which would hold the screen, was inserted. Occasionally Jake would experience the disconcerting sensation of his stoper, which was chewing steadily away at solid rock far overhead deep in the back, suddenly jumping ahead a few inches, a sure sign that it had just drilled a "slip"—a gap between layers of otherwise solid rock—and that was truly scary. It meant that a huge chunk of loose was suspended over their heads. At that size even the most diligent and experienced scaler could be deceived—the loose was so large it would ring true—like good ground. A chunk of loose that size, should it ever break free, would burst through the screen, and come crashing down onto the floor of the stope, crushing everything in its path in an instant. Jake had no illusions about the consequences, and mostly he tried not to think about them too much. One day, though, he asked Bob about it as they ate their lunch.

"Do you ever think about it?"

"'Bout what?"

Jake pointed up at the back. Both of them knew he meant the ever-present spectre of sure, sudden death that was suspended just over their heads.

"Sure, I think about it ..."

"And?"

"I try to look on the bright side." Bob chewed his sandwich reflectively. "If one a' them big chunks ever did come down, we'd never know what hit us. Not a bad way to go ..."

"But how would they get us out? Wouldn't someone wonder what happened to us?"

"Oh, sure, the Mine Rescue guys would come in, maybe use an air bag to lift the chunk off us. We'd prob'ly come out—if we ever did come out—in pieces."

Jake shivered at the notion that this dank and eternally dark space could become his final resting place for eternity.

"So—so why do you keep doing it, Bob?"

"What, mining, you mean?"

Jake nodded.

Bob shrugged. "Look, kid. This is what I do. Where else can a guy with a Grade Two education make this kind of money? I own a house, my wife and kids don't want for nothin', I've even got a little put away so my kids can go to college and never have to face this," he lifted his eyebrows in the direction of the chancey back. "And besides, it gets in your blood. Not everyone can do what we do. And what about you? You got what, Grade Eleven?"

"Ten," Jake confessed.

"Yeah, and next year the village idiot graduates, and you ain't shit ..."

Bob paused. "Whether we like it or not, we're in a war down here. The company won't admit it, or the politicians, but that's a fact. More men have been killed in Ontario's hard rock mines over the years than in some whole wars Canada's fought. No one even knows how many. But, for sure, there's been hundreds killed right here in the Sudbury camp alone."

"So why do people keep doing it?"

Bob smiled ruefully and rubbed his thumb and fingers together in the universal sign for money ... "Speaking of which ..." Bob stood up and brushed the sandwich crumbs from his overalls.

Jake needed no further prompting. They were on a roll now—hundred twenty five percent bonus in the bank, maybe a hundred fifty, even—they wouldn't know for sure until the engineer came down to officially measure their total push several days from now.

As the pay period wore on fall descended toward winter, forcing Jake and Bob to steel themselves increasingly against the gathering cold in their stope. Nevertheless they continued to drill, blast, scale, roof bolt and screen their way through the parlous rubble heap that was Frood Mine's Upper Country. Thanks to Bob's experience and leadership, and in no small measure to Jake's muscle and youthful energy, the duo made steady headway, banking the bonus at a prodigious rate that pleased them both.

At long last the day of reckoning arrived. Time to redeem the bonus bank. Bob led the way to the shift supervisor's office, and Jake was happy to let him do the talking.

Soon enough the three of them were trudging their way back down the drift, and as soon as they entered the stope Jake had the sense something was wrong.

It was way too bright, for one thing, and the cold was even more intense than ever, not least because of the breeze that was now whistling through their stope. Breeze? Jake stopped short at the sight. It was gone! The whole heading had disappeared, jackleg and all, as if it had never existed! The screen overhead was buckled and at the front end it dangled down crazily, screening them off from nothing more than daylight and birdsong. At first Bob was as dumbfounded as Jake by this unexpected turn of events, but soon he started to laugh uncontrollably as he began to comprehend that the cross shift's blast had broken through into the pit, and that their precious, hard-won bonus bank—probably thousands of dollars' worth of it—braces for Bob's kids' teeth, the guitar lessons Jake had planned so that he could finally master Ben's old Gibson, all their heart's desires—were now nothing more than worthless rubble lying beneath the mangled jackleg that dangled on its hoses, suspended over the water that covered the bottom of the old Frood Open Pit.

Bob was laughing so hard he had to retreat back into the stope and sit down on the muck pile. He tried over and over to say something, but every attempt brought on another laughing fit that left him gasping for breath, and slapping his knees.

Jake felt sick. How was it possible that the solid rock they had drilled, the tons of loose they had dodged, could disappear into thin air, as if it had never existed?

The shift supervisor was coming to the same conclusion. He was already smiling his tight little smile.

"Well, fellas that's it, then. Can't pay for push that ain't there. Sorry." He shook his head and headed back for the cage.

Finally Bob, still on the muck pile, got a grip. "Sorry 'bout this, partner." Then he stood up. "Better get a move on, bid us into a new heading."

But Jake was still incredulous at this sudden turn of events. "But—but is that all there is? There must be more—"

"More? No, partner there really isn't. We got outta this shithole in one piece. There's your bonus." There was a cold, almost triumphant gleam in Bob's eyes, which were startlingly blue now, seen in the unaccustomed light of day.

And then he was gone.

Jake took Bob's place on the muck pile. Alone now, he shivered in the cold. It was late October, and the cold was more penetrating each morning.

Even here the smell of snow was in the air.

Jake took one more look around, sighed, and shook his head in disbelief.

Skating rink in hell.

PART FOUR

Into the Middle Country

21

An Offer They Couldn't Refuse

Bob's maniacal laughter in the face of disaster would baffle Jake for months—rankle, in fact—but he didn't broach the subject with his partner when Bob returned, at last, to the heading. He'd been gone for a few hours, in fact, but to Jake it felt like an eternity—hours of prime bonus-earning time wasted.

"Well?" Jake demanded impatiently, jumping up from the muck pile.

"Oh, partner ..." was all Bob said, shaking his head as he took Jake's place.

"What took you? Do we have a new stope?"

"Hold on there, young feller. What took me was I had to go all the way to the mine super, and yes we have a new stope. But it's not that simple ..."

"Well where is it? C'mon. let's go! We've wasted half a shift here, Bob! Pitter-patter let's get at 'er!"

"Will you wait a goddamned minute? You need to hear this ... To begin with, the stope's right here, just down a few levels, enough to get us below the pit, and outta this cold. But that's not all ..."

Jake swallowed and nodded expectantly. He was all ears now.

"Listen, they want us to start taking much bigger cuts, see? Fourteen by sixteen 'stead of eight by eight."

"*What?* Why? That'll mean way more drilling for us just to make our reg'lar push!"

"Listen to me now—everythin's about to change, whether we like it or not. They're bringin' in a whole new mining method, with a whole bunch a' new machinery—big stuff—that won't fit into the usual headings. Damndest thing I ever heard of—biggest thing is these new trammers—they'll run on diesel, and tires ..."

"Diesel!" Jake snorted in disbelief. "Why just the exhaust fumes'll kill us! Underground?"

Bob nodded. "They know that. They plan to boost ventilation. New raises, bigger blower motors, the lot."

Jake frowned. It was all beginning to sink in. "Wow! That *is* big. Trackless mining. But if they're as big as you say, how'll they even get them underground?"

Bob shrugged. "Break 'em down on surface and sling the parts down beneath the cage, reassemble 'em underground."

"Trackless mining ..." Jake repeated. The wheels were turning now. "No more laying track, always having to extend it down the drifts ..."

Bob nodded. "And not only that, eventually we'd come to ramp mining. Don't you see? No more shaft. Just drive a ramp down, and you could drive these new trammers right underground ..."

"Too much ... and what's all this got to do with us?"

"That's just it! They want us to go first! To start mining with these new dimensions!"

Jake wasn't sure he shared Bob's new-found enthusiasm. "But what'll it mean for our bonus? With all that extra drilling ..."

"Well, I just cut a deal with the mine super himself. He guarantees the new rates'll be set to work out at our usual rate, maybe even more. They really want *us* to start this, Jake."

Still the younger man remained nonplussed. "You sure we can trust 'em, Bob?"

"No, not entirely," Jesperson conceded. "But if it don't play out next pay period, then we're outta there, and I told him so. We'll bid in to someplace else. Okay?"

Jake sighed. "I guess so. But I just keep wondering 'What's the catch?'"

As the duo repaired to the drift to locate their new workplace neither man could know the immense ramifications of what they were about to undertake, or that, because of it, things would never be quite the same ever again.

22

Cracks, Slips, Fissures and Gaps

Instead of confronting Bob with his disappointment at his partner's seemingly cavalier attitude toward the loss of the bonus bank, Jake took the matter to heart, quietly nursing his disappointment, knowing that it was a lesser wound compared to the heartbreak of Ben's death, and of his rupture with Jo Ann. Those hurts were real and ongoing, and perhaps it was the need to lose himself in something greater that drew Jake inexorably back into the affairs of Local 598, now more embattled than ever.

Gilpin, too, remained on the scene, churning out a steady stream of leaflets, broadsides, newspaper display ads and thirty-second radio spots in an effort to stem the barrage of anti-Mine Mill propaganda that flooded the city's airwaves and newspaper pages as the raids dragged on.

The battle for the hearts and minds of Sudbury's miners and surface plant workers raged on for yet another season with first one side gaining ground, only to lose it in the face of a determined counter-attack from the other.

There were Mine Mill hold-outs—Frood Mine was one such—and Steelworker strongholds—Stobie, right next to Frood, provided counterbalance. Many of Mine Mill's adherents were proving fiercely loyal to their old union—the only one they had ever known, after all—despite the disastrous defeat of '58. Divisions on the job were acrimonious. And the fissures were about more than politics.

Even now no one is certain when it began, who came first. Some will contend that it was Jake himself that May morning in 1963 when he first stumbled off the cage onto the 2200 foot level of Garson Mine.

If so, he was the leading edge of a demographic wave that was about to swamp the city, above ground and below. And, as the decade wore on, what first appeared as a fissure would soon widen into a crack, and then become a gap. They arrived in wave after wave of mass hirings that accompanied the boom that presaged the Vietnam War. In every mine, on every level, their presence was unmistakeable—"the young guys"— bringing their own music, mores and culture that were destined to revolutionize both the union, and the broader social context.

They were a scruffy lot, but smart and better educated (Grade 12 had become the new educational gold standard for Inco recruiters.)

"The old guys" of Bob Jesperson's generation were dubious about this new breed—dubious about their ability to withstand the rigours of life underground, dubious about their ability to do the work—and it was true that in every batch of new hires there was always one or two who would arrive on the level, take a quick, wide-eyed look around, quietly grab his lunch box and take the cage back to surface, never to be seen again.

But the vast majority, lured by the promise of rich bonus earnings, sucked it up and partnered up with the old guys who would teach them the rudiments and show them how to finish a shift in one piece. Young guys like David Patterson, Keith Lovely, Kenny Mersel, Harvey Wyers and Ron Dupuis—this many were at Frood Mine alone—were destined to transform not only the union, but the community writ large.

The company, meanwhile, observed the proliferating factionalism—especially the Mine Mill-Steel divide—with quiet satisfaction. Officially the company pronounced itself neutral in the bitter Steelworker raids on Mine Mill, a stance Jake and Gilpin had seen firsthand to be a sham. Always in public the company pronounced itself above the fray, abruptly terminating negotiations over a new contract: it was up to their workers to elect which union would speak on their behalf, at which time the company would return to the table.

And, in a very real sense, this was true. The Steel raiders were working towards just such a vote in their untiring efforts to sign up new members right under the noses of Spike Sworski and the Mine Mill leadership.

The Steelworkers would need to sign up a clear majority of the workforce to successfully apply to force a government-supervised vote as to which union should represent the Sudbury workforce. And nor would a simple fifty-percent-plus-one suffice.

There were bound to be scores of challenges from the Mine Mill side, many of which would be upheld. It was a daunting task, to sign up eight thousand or so workers to new Steelworkers' membership on the job in the face of such open Mine Mill hostility, but the effort gained traction, garnering new adherents with each passing day. The steady stream of anti-Mine Mill, anti-Communist invective from pulpit, newspaper and radio loudspeaker took a toll, and the Steelworkers controlled the timetable. They could apply for a government-supervised vote when they were confident they had a healthy margin of newly signed membership cards in hand, and not one moment before. In the meantime the number of signed cards and the identities of their key organizers remained a closely guarded secret.

Jake drifted back into the Mine Mill Hall in November. He found the upstairs offices, the sanctum sanctorum of the leadership, a changed place. The smell of stale cigarette smoke was now all-pervasive, and the place fairly vibrated with tension. It also seemed shabbier than he'd remembered, lived in. Jake immediately sought out Gilpin.

He found his old confidante in a bare office, pounding away on his typewriter.

"Hey Foley! How goes the battle? Surprised you're still here."

Gilpin greeted him with a wan smile and a shrug. "I quit the paper. Decided this was where I belong. I'll sink or swim with my brothers and sisters of the Mine Mill."

"Very noble of you, Foley. And how's all that working out for ya?"

Gilpin gestured at the palpable tension that surrounded his cubicle.

"Oh, as you see. Good days and bad. And nobility had very little to do with it, by the way. I decided it was time to stop just writing about the CIA, and time to start *doing* something."

"Sure looks like you're still writing ..."

Gilpin grunted. "Yeah, but now it's for the union, against the CIA. No more pretending to be objective."

"So you're still convinced they're behind this mess?"

Gilpin nodded. "Sorry to hear about your father-in-law."

"Father-in-law to be. Maybe." Jake corrected.

"What happened to him?"

"Hit by a bus crossing the street."

"And how is such a thing even possible? Those buses are huge, and painted that god-awful orange ..."

Jake looked down, trying to suppress a laugh. It was true. All the buses in the city's transit fleet, like all city-owned vehicles, were painted an ugly, garish orange. When he looked up again, he could see that Gilpin was struggling to suppress his own mirth. "Well, he *was* very near-sighted," Jake offered, and suddenly both of them were roaring with laughter.

"So you don't think it was just an accident?" Jake asked Gilpin after he'd caught his breath.

"I think the man knew too much. He was in the middle of way too much shit. In over his head."

"Or maybe he just took one for the team."

"Meaning?"

"Well, think about it, Foley. We see him when we bust in that day, but he also sees me. So maybe he worries I'll tell Jo Ann. And how's that gonna play out? That he's in cahoots with the guy who's just killed my brother—is my girlfriend gonna have to choose between her boyfriend and her own father? And maybe he's not sure who she is gonna choose, so ..."

"So he falls on his sword, looks for the final exit. And takes it."

"And what about you, Foley? You still convinced the CIA is behind all this?"

" Oh Lord yes, more so now than ever. Have you heard the latest?"

"Try me."

"You know about this new university that's starting up over the other side of Lake Ramsey?"

"Of course." Everyone in town had heard about the new institution, the city's first seat of university-level post-secondary learning, founded by a sizeable donation from International Nickel. At the moment it was little more than a muddy construction site and a cluster of loosely federated, self-declared colleges, each with an affiliation to one religious denomination or another.

"Well," Gilpin continued with a frown, "there's something fishy going on over there."

"Oh yeah? In what way?"

"It's at the Jesuit's college, the University of Sudbury. There's a new priest out there who's just dropped in outta nowhere, teaching this special night course aimed at Mine Mill members, and their wives. All about how the union's run by Communists, and how we're a threat to the entire Free World ..."

"Sounds like the usual red-baiting bullshit to me," Jake shrugged.

"Oh, it is. But this guy's *good*. As if it's not enough we got the priests in their pulpits preaching sermons against us every Sunday, and that Tory rag the *Sudbury Star* takin' shots every chance they get, now Inco donates five million bucks to start up a new university and right away this new priest just happens to land in here—some guy no one's ever heard of—and the Jesuits have a cockpit to help mastermind the raids ..." Gilpin shook his head in exasperation. "Well, Jake, I'm on deadline ..."

Jake hastily excused himself, and went off in search of Spike Sworski.

He found the union president in his office. The door was open, but Jake tapped lightly on the door frame before entering. "Hello, Mr. Sworski," he ventured.

The union president was engrossed in reading a file on his desk. He glanced up over his reading glasses before breaking into a broad smile. "Jake McCool! This *is* a surprise! Come in, come in!"

"How's the knee?"

"Oh, it's fine." Jake said with a shrug. "I've been back at work for almost a month now. How're you holding up, Mr. Sworski?"

"Winning some and losing some, it seems. What are you hearing out there on the job?"

"Well, I'm at Frood right now—support's pretty solid, sir."

Sworski nodded. "God bless the Frood Miners …
Would that we had ten more mines like it …"

"But we don't?"

"On a good day, maybe five."

Jake whistled. "Only five out of ten? Is it really that
close?"

Sworski wagged his head from side to side, pursing
his lips. "Maybe. Who knows? The only thing we
know for sure is that Steel is continuing to sign more
cards, and coming at us from every direction."

"Any idea when the vote'll be?"

Sworski turned his hands palms up. "That, too, is
out of our hands."

Jake studied the union leader closely. Sworski was
still well dressed, dapper as ever, but there was an air
about him—melancholic, brooding, almost fatalis-
tic—that Jake had never noticed before.

Jake also noticed something else he hadn't seen
before—a pair of expensive, high-powered binoculars on Spike's desk.

"Taking up bird watching?" he motioned toward
the field glasses.

"Not hardly," the union leader replied with a sardonic grin. "Figure we're always being watched—
might as well watch back! No, but seriously, I do enjoy
watching the sporting events over at Queen's, the ice
skating and such."

Jake nodded. During the winter months, he knew,
the running track at Queen's Athletic Field was
flooded by the City Parks and Rec Department, the
oval converted into one of the city's most popular
outdoor skating venues.

"Well, I won't keep you, sir ..." Jake ducked out, and returned directly to Gilpin's little cubicle, to share his concerns about their mutual friend.

"Hey, what's up with Spike?"

Gilpin looked up from his typewriter with a frown.

"Spike senses he's going down ..."

"Really! Is he?"

"He might be ... A lot of rank-and-filers still blame him for what happened in '58 ..."

"Wow! Spike Sworski defeated as president of 598! It hardly seems possible ..."

"Oh, it's possible, kid. Election's next month. Better get used to the idea, although I don't like it anymore'n you do ..."

"What? But who?"

"Oh, Hoople and that gang, is who. Suspicions are that Steel is behind 'em, but no one knows for sure."

"Aww, no! But that'd mean the end of the Local!"

"Afraid so. Now you know why he looks so worried. And it's not just the presidency, either. There's a whole slate of 'em running—Vice, Treasurer ..."

Jake withdrew in stunned silence.

His mind raced on the long drive home to the Valley. First the disastrous defeat of '58 ... Now, maybe the election of a secretly pro-Steel faction to head up the big Local ... What did it all mean? And, more to the point, what would happen next?

23

Terra Incognita

Jake was eager to discuss the latest news with Bob once they took a break in their new heading. So far, the work was going as Bob had predicted: at the end of their first pay period their bonus had remained well into the hundred percent range, and they were well below the bottom of the pit—a good thing, as November had arrived and with it Sudbury's skies had turned a steady, sullen overcast—usually a precursor of the year's first snowfall.

In fact, if anything, the new stope was a tad on the warmish side. And occasionally the acrid smell of sulphur smoke was evident from the fire burning down below, deep in the bowels of Frood Mine's high grade Bottom Country.

"Sworski in trouble!" Bob marvelled when Jake told him the news. "Well I must say I'm not surprised." As an active shop steward, charged with enforcing the collective bargaining agreement on the job at all times, Bob had more than a passing interest in developments at the Union Hall.

"But a slate of Hoople's cronies? I'm not sure I like the sound of that …"

Bob's sentiments echoed those of Big Bill, who had feared the worst after Jake shared his news at the dinner table.

"Yeah, well I can tell ya Sworski himself looked pretty worried," Jake reported.

"Then I'll work extra hard to pull the vote around here," Bob vowed as he brought the lunch break to an abrupt end. That was one disadvantage to the new heading—much more drilling was required due to the new, more spacious dimensions, so lunchtime was curtailed.

Another was the height of the back. The roof of the new heading was much higher now, making the back much more difficult to see, and to scale. The only solution was to scrape the muck pile as high as possible, and to use it as a crude staging, standing atop it to inspect the back, and to scale, and to prop up the stoper for drilling holes for the roofbolts.

It was tedious, but they learned to adapt.

And, as promised, the bonus was good.

On the Friday morning of the last day of the second pay period in their new stope, Bob met Jake at the cage. "Listen, I've got a meeting," he told Jake. "Why don't you go on ahead and tidy up in the stope as best you can?"

Although they worked now as equals, there was little doubt that the older, more experienced miner was, in fact, the leader of the team.

"Sure," Jake answered without hesitation.

The two men separated and soon Jake was on his own in the stope. It felt eerie—and strangely quiet—without Bob, but Jake busied himself as best he could, scaling the back and carefully arranging the tools in preparation for the day's drilling to begin.

At last, with the heading ship shape, Jake scooped out a seat on the muck pile and sat down to await Bob's arrival. It rarely happened that he was alone in the stope, and Jake found himself listening to sounds that were normally drowned out by the roar of the jackleg—the steady drip of water, the hissing of the air line and the muted roar of a jackleg in some distant heading. And then, so faint at first that he wasn't sure it wasn't his imagination, Jake thought he heard something strange—wholly unfamiliar in the far off distance. Indistinct though it was, it was steady.

Gradually the sound grew louder. It was definitely real, Jake concluded. Soon the sound had become an identifiable noise—a steady chug-a-chug-a-chug sound. Whatever it was, it was headed this way.

Jake was almost alarmed when he saw something he'd never seen before: his own shadow dancing on the wall of the stope! He jumped to his feet at once, and turned to face whatever it was entering the heading, only to be blinded by the glare of headlights. Shielding his eyes with his hands Jake could just make out a miner's cap lamp above and behind the headlights.

It was, Jake soon realized, Bob. He was standing on a platform in the middle of this new contraption, intently manipulating a bank of levers in front of him. With no little difficulty Bob guided the machine, which travelled on rubber tires, around the muck pile and into a precise location facing the breast. Once he was satisfied with the location Bob turned off the engine and stepped down from his platform in the middle of his new machine, which looked to Jake like an ungainly agglomeration of hoses, metal and some kind of chassis riding above conventional rubber tires.

"What the—?" Jake exploded.

Bob gestured proudly at the machine. "This here's the first three-boom jumbo drill in all of Frood Mine! Here, give us a hand…" Bob moved quickly to disconnect the air line from the jackleg and to snap it on to the new machine.

Jake dutifully assisted by helping to drag the heavy air hose across the jagged floor of the stope.

Bob re-ascended his low platform and, with much hissing of pressurized air, began manipulating levers once again. A bank of floodlights illuminated the bizarre scene. Jake watched as the machine began to unfold, revealing, finally, something that was familiar to Jake—three jacklegs attached to articulating metal arms. It was a robot! Bob placed the tips of drill steels carefully, with much trial and error, just so against the breast.

"Here, you'll be needin' this." He handed Jake a hard hat with two strange bumps on the sides. Jake examined the hat, quickly realizing the bumps were ear muffs that swung down over his ears.

With that Bob opened the air to the drills and Jake watched as three jacklegs began to turn simultaneously. The whole spectacle was illuminated in the glare of floodlights which had also unfolded from the machine. It was the most light Jake had ever seen in one place underground. The roar of the three drills must have been deafening, but the ear muffs filtered out most of the racket.

"It's like a robot!" Jake yelled to Bob, who bobbed his head in agreement.

"Does the work of three men." Bob wasn't shouting, and Jake realized the ear muffs muffled the noise of the drills, but not speech.

"Six men," he frowned. "Two to a drill."

They finished the shift, their round drilled, with no incident and even less effort. Even Jake, dubious as he was at this experiment, was impressed—they had finished drilling *before* lunch, which allowed for a leisurely break and left them with only loading their rounds to do in the afternoon. They barely broke a sweat. If they kept this up, Jake reckoned, their bonus earnings would be through the roof. The approaching holidays should be most bountiful in both the McCool and Jesperson households this year.

But everything turned on a dime when they reached the cage.

"Guess you fellas didn't hear what just happened down in the States—Kennedy got killed!" the tender announced. He was bringing the news, he realized, to some of the very last people on the planet—certainly the continent—to get wind of it.

"What?"

"Where?"

"Down in Dallas."

"But how—are they sure he's dead?"

"Oh, they're sure, all right. Cronkite himself announced it an hour, hour-and-a-half ago. They figure it was some kind of high-powered rifle."

When he reached surface, Jake discovered someone had jury-rigged an old black-and-white portable TV in the shaft house. He paused to watch the coverage.

It looked like it had been a bright, sunny day down in Dallas. The grainy black-and-white images were shown over and over—the presidential motorcade passing by, the President and First Lady in an open-air black Lincoln convertible, both of them happily waving to the crowds, and then, suddenly, something indistinct happened in the car, and someone in a dark suit—presumably a Secret Service agent—was scrambling to climb into the President's car from the rear over the trunk lid, Jackie Kennedy, her arm outstretched, was trying to pull him aboard, and then the front part of the motorcade, including the big black Lincoln, accelerated and pulled away, out of sight. The President had been shot, the announcer intoned somberly, and had been taken to Parkland Hospital in Dallas for emergency surgery.

Then Walter Cronkite appeared. President Kennedy, he announced, was dead. After he said that, Cronkite, appearing overwhelmed at the news, removed his eyeglasses and looked away from the cameras.

The TV set was no hell, the reception was even worse, and occasionally a passer-by would stop to fiddle with the set's rabbit ears to try to pull in a better signal, but Jake stood, mesmerized, and watched the afternoon's events as they were played over and over.

Eventually he came to his senses and headed for the dry.

Even in the familiar surroundings of the shower room with the near scalding-hot water hitting his skin like tiny needles and the steam beginning to rise around him, Jake felt weird. Between the new drill and the day's events down in Dallas he sensed he was on the verge of some strange new world.

24

Halftime Show

The rest of the weekend remained gloomy and chilly, threatening snow, but the snow would not come—only a cold rain blowing in on a north wind beneath the swiftly scudding, leaden clouds—and so Foley Gilpin and Spike Sworski were both grateful for the respite provided by the Canadian Football League semi-final game that Sunday afternoon.

It was, quite literally, the only game in town. The big American television networks had decided to continue their coverage of the Kennedy assassination and pre-empt the day's roster of National Football League games, but the executives of the Canadian Broadcasting Corporation elected to televise the Canadian game—JFK wasn't *their* President, after all—a national distinction that was heartily welcomed by both men that gloomy Sunday afternoon.

Anyone inclined to credit the slanderous accusations made by the Steel raiders against Sworski that he had somehow benefitted improperly from union funds during his tenure as Local 598 president should simply visit his friend's house, Gilpin reflected.

A modest storey-and-a-half bungalow on a hill overlooking the Coniston smelter, Spike's residence, which he had inherited from his father, was unprepossessing in the extreme. Still, on this chill and gloomy November afternoon it was a warm and welcoming refuge in a world that seemed to be spinning madly out of control.

Foley had settled comfortably in front of the TV set with a cold beer, still intent on learning the intricacies of Canadian football, at once so similar—and yet so different—compared with the American game to which he was accustomed. There was no doubt that the overall talent level was inferior up here north of the border—the players were all NFL rejects, after all—but Foley, long a Bears fan, found himself intrigued with the nuanced differences in the Canadian game—the larger field, the extra player on both sides of the football, and, most of all the fact that offences were allowed only three attempts, rather than four, to advance the football ten yards for a first down. Logically, the Canadian rules should have militated against high-scoring games. Instead, as Foley was learning, the Canadian games were often wildly wide-open, high-scoring affairs that reminded him of the sandlot touch football games of his youth. The product was often a game that was more entertaining than its much more bally-hooed, over-hyped NFL counterpart; or at least that was Spike's contention, and Foley wasn't so sure his friend wasn't right.

Even as the Americans mourned the shocking death of their charismatic young President, Canadians had life-and-death political issues of their own: all eyes were turned to the Prairie province of Saskatchewan, where Premier Tommy Douglas had, a year earlier, introduced a provincially funded medicare scheme intended to provide free medical care to everyone in the province. The move had proved hugely controversial, especially among Saskatchewan's doctors who feared the plan would ensnare them in a web of bureaucratic red tape and perhaps even impose a cap on their lucrative salaries. They threatened to strike in protest, but Douglas stood his ground. The battle lines were drawn, and the nation held its breath. Here in Spike's living room, opinion was decidedly mixed on the matter. While no one sided with the doctors, Douglas's party, the Cooperative Commonwealth Federation, or CCF, aroused strong emotions because of its close working relationship with the United Steelworkers of America. The CCF, a social democratic party, was in competition with the Communist Party of Canada for the allegiance—and sometimes the votes—of progressive Canadians. This sectarian feuding on the left often became bitter and vitriolic, and this, too, was an element in the Steel raids in Sudbury. Because the party was the political bedfellow of Steel, both Foley and Sworski adopted a healthy skepticism when it came to the CCF.

And so when an announcer for CBC News interrupted the game for "A Special News Bulletin" both Gilpin and Sworski expected it would concern Saskatchewan, but, the announcer concluded "We are joining our American affiliate, NBC News, to bring you the late breaking developments in the Kennedy assassination ..."

"What's this now?" Gilpin sat upright. Sworski hurried back from the kitchen, reaching behind the TV set to stop the picture from rolling uncontrollably.

"We take you now to Dallas, where the man suspected of shooting and killing President Kennedy was himself gunned down just moments ago. The videotape you are about to see was provided to us courtesy of NBC Television News ..."

Another announcer's voice took over the narration on the videotape. "Here he comes now," the announcer said as Oswald was led into the room by a pair of burly Dallas cops in white Stetsons who towered over the slender, almost waif-like, handcuffed figure. Then something dark appeared in the bottom right of the screen, Oswald flinched, and then winced, and disappeared from view. "He's been shot!" The announcer's voice rang out. "Lee Harvey Oswald's been shot!"

Gilpin was out of his chair in an instant, headed for the door. He began to struggle into his overcoat and galoshes.

"Hey! Where ya goin'? What about the game?" demanded Sworski, startled by his friend's sudden reflex actions.

"I dunno, man," was all Gilpin could answer, as he shrugged into his coat. "But I gotta go."

And that was very much the truth—Foley Gilpin had no idea where he was going. But he hurried to his car and backed out of Sworski's driveway before ever stopping to think about that.

Where *was* he going? He headed toward town, toward his apartment, still too dazed to think much about what he was doing. He turned on the radio, feverishly twisting the tuning knob, in search of the latest news from Dallas, which was pouring in. Oswald had been taken to Parkland Hospital for emergency medical treatment, the same place Kennedy had been taken just two days earlier. His assailant had been immediately wrestled to the ground and arrested. He had already been identified as Jack Ruby, a Dallas nightclub owner. The story was breaking very fast as Gilpin drove down the hill from Sworski's and turned onto the back road to the city, a narrow twisting route that ran through a narrow defile between black, rocky hills, studded with skeletal birch and poplar, their branches stripped bare by the cold wind and drizzle that was falling even now. The way led through a random scattering of modest houses and a rail siding—less than a village—called Rumford.

News reports indicated that Oswald was being led away for questioning at the time of the shooting. Clearly someone hadn't wanted him to talk, Gilpin surmised.

When he entered his apartment, Foley Gilpin was surprised to hear his phone ringing. He'd made very few new friends in the city, and certainly the Union Hall would be closed today.

"Hello, I'm looking for Foley Gilpin," said a familiar voice as Gilpin picked up the handset.

"This is Foley," he answered.

"Foley, old friend, this is Hildy!"

"Hildy!" Gilpin was astonished to hear the voice of his former colleague. But now there was something new in that normally breezy self-confident voice—an undertone of self-doubt, even—perhaps of supplication.

"Uh Foley ... Look, I know you're no longer at the paper, but I wonder if I might have a moment of your time?

"Can you tell me everything you know about the CIA?"

PART FIVE

Insurgents in Power

Queen's Athletic Park (Oryst Sawchuk)

25

Insurgents In Power

Even as heart-rending tragedy—the funeral of a President, the farewell salute of John-John to his father, the lighting of the Eternal Flame at Arlington—continued to unfold before a sorrowing nation glued to the television, in a nation to the north the countdown continued on Spike Sworski's term of office.

The pros and cons of Sworski's five-year tenure were played out in a visceral, often downright nasty, leaflet and rumour campaign that brought little credit to either side. A whisper campaign had it that Sworski was a closet Communist—or at the very least a fellow-traveller—who had secretly grown rich during the '58 strike, even as strikers and their families were reduced to rooting for potatoes just to have enough to eat. Hoople and his cronies, the other side countered, were really nothing more than Steelworker shills, concealing their real allegiance until there was no turning back. Once their true colours were revealed, the big Local's dues dollars would begin to flow south, to Yankeeland, out of the members' control, never to be seen again by the Sudbury rank and file.

The snow came, finally, on election day, the usual first snowfall: heavy, wet stuff that delights school kids and vexes their parents as they hassle with snow-clogged streets and tire chains.

Despite the weather the voter turnout was heavy at the ballot boxes which had been placed in every shaft house and surface plant across the Basin.

As they came off shift, individuals who comprised the great, roistering mass of the Sudbury rank and file stood patiently in line, awaiting their chance to cast a vote that would determine the fate of the largest union local the country had ever seen. They waited, for the most part, without complaint even though they were anxious to leave the workplace for the day, and were losing precious minutes in the comfort of home with their wives and children. This day had been a long time coming, and each was moved, by spite or solidarity, to have his say in the selection of his Local Union leadership for the next five years.

As the lines cleared and the early gloom of December descended over the Basin, the city waited with bated breath, anxious to learn the outcome of a titanic struggle that had split it down the middle for so long, a microcosmic version of a global conflict in which the fate of all humankind weighed in the balance.

Jake gulped down a hasty dinner before racing back into town, to the Union Hall, where he knew the first results would be reported. The second floor was packed, abuzz with tension, and filled with reporters, most of them very young—not much older than Jake. He found Sworski pacing endlessly, chain-smoking, looking pale and drawn, fearing the worst.

The early returns put Spike handily in the lead, but they were all from Frood. The race tightened as results from the other mines that sprawled across the Sudbury Basin poured in over the next several hours. Then the count from the surface plants came flooding in, and Spike's early lead was obliterated. By eleven o'clock he was down by a thousand votes and the matter, as the most percipient observers knew, was all but decided. The union secretaries who'd also come in to watch the results were red-eyed and shocked, watching in stunned silence as the future of their workplace began to shift before their eyes. President, vice-president, treasurer, recording secretary, all their bosses, were changing literally overnight. Who were these new individuals? What would they be like to work for? Suddenly uncertainty was the order of the day.

And then, just before midnight, it was all over. There were no more votes to count. Spike and his entire slate had been swept out of office by a wave of rank-and-file discontent. Spike retreated to his office, the secretaries departed for home and the reporters hurried off to file their stories.

Foley Gilpin surveyed the shambles of overflowing ashtrays and abandoned coffee cups that littered the suddenly deserted floor.

"Wanna go for a beer?" he turned to Jake.

"Sure. Where?"

"Downstairs?"

"Okay. What about him?" Jake motioned toward the closed door of Sworski's office.

"Just a minute—I'll go see." Gilpin disappeared into Spike's office. He re-emerged moments later, looking sombre.

"Should we turn off the lights?" Jake was heading for the stairs.

"Nah, let him do it."

"Will the last member of Mine Mill please turn off the lights, eh?"

Gilpin merely grunted at Jake's attempt at gallows humour and followed him down the stairs.

The bar in the Mine Mill Hall was in the basement, a spartan, high-ceilinged, strictly utilitarian space dedicated to the serious consumption of beer, and to the conversation that came with it. It was a largely male preserve restricted to union members and their guests, whose names were pencilled into an imposing ledger book kept beside the bar. Jake signed Foley in and they settled in with their drinks.

"How's he taking it?" Jake looked upwards to indicate the executive offices two floors above.

"Oh, pretty hard. Why wouldn't he?"

Jake shook his head. "I still can't believe it. Why did it happen, do you think, Foley?"

"Oh, '58, I think. The rank and file just never forgave him for that ... and, of course the smear campaign didn't help, either ... That, and Spike does have his arrogant side, you know."

Jake frowned at this criticism of a man who they both considered a friend. It felt like kicking a man while he was down.

"Oh, come on, Jake, you know it's true—look at the way he'd shut down any dissent at the membership meetings. Those things have a way of catching up with you."

"So what'll happen now do you think?"

To Jake's surprise Foley responded by making a slashing gesture across his own throat.

"Really? They'll let you go? After you quit your job down in the States and all?"

Gilpin smiled ruefully. "Worst career decision of all time. But yeah, I'm a goner. I'm just way too close to Spike. They know that ..."

"Gee, that's tough. Sorry to hear it, Foley. So what'll you do now?"

Gilpin shrugged. "I'm not sure. Maybe some free-lancing. I hear through the grapevine the *Globe's* always looking for a reliable Sudbury stringer ..."

Jake nodded, impressed. The *Toronto Globe and Mail* was one of Canada's best papers, the closest thing Canada had to the *New York Times*.

"And so what happens to the Local?"

"I'm not much of a betting man, but if I was, I'd bet we won't be sitting here five years from now. In some other Union Hall, maybe, but not this one."

"Shit. We *need* this union!"

"Oh, there'll still be a union, just not *this* union."

Foley looked abruptly at his watch. "Well kid, I'm not much looking forward to the morning after upstairs, but I guess I better be there …" He reached for the draft glass in front of him, drained it and slammed it back down on the table in quiet emphasis.

The action shook Jake out of his reverie about the future, and he reached out for his own glass and finished his beer.

"Yeah, and I've got an early cage … Need a ride?"

"Naw, I can walk home, thanks."

And with that the two men parted, to make their separate ways through the snowy streets of Sudbury.

As with any community tethered to the exigencies of a continuously producing heavy industry through the umbilical of labour, the working day in Sudbury begins at an ungodly early hour.

The McCool household was no exception. The morning after the union election found its occupants stirring well before dawn—Big Bill out to get his morning papers, Jake sleepily reaching for his first cup of coffee, Alice preparing to start the breakfast that would power her son through a morning of heavy labour underground.

It was still pitch dark outside as Jake took his place at the kitchen table and his father settled in beside him with the newspapers, still redolent of cold air and printer's ink and fresh newsprint. Rising super early so that he could catch an early morning cage was a habit Big Bill had never broken, even in his retirement years.

"Too bad about Spike, huh?" Jake ventured to his father.

The big man only grunted as he scanned the front page of *The Toronto Star.*

"And how is Spike?" Big Bill asked finally, peering over the top of his paper.

"Taking it pretty hard."

"Sorry to hear it."

Jake knew that was true.

"He's paying the price for that strike," Alice chimed in from the kitchen.

"True," agreed Big Bill.

"But Dad, you told me once that he had no choice— that he was carrying out the will of the membership," protested Jake.

"Ye-es, but the company forced the issue, made us strike when *they* wanted a strike. Spike was caught in between. Terrible timing. Classic squeeze play."

Jake finished his coffee and pushed away from the table. He grabbed his lunch pail as he passed through the kitchen and bussed his mother on the cheek.

"Bye, Mum."

"Bye, Son," Alice replied, adding, as she did every day, "Work safe."

And then Jake was out the back door and into the dark and the cold and snow, which managed to be both slightly slippery and sticky underfoot at the same time.

No time was wasted before the transfer of power at the Mine Mill Hall. That very night, in fact, the newly elected officers were sworn in—insurgents no more.

So important was this ritual that the National Office flew in a high-ranking national official to administer the oath of office. The framed Charter of Local 598 was taken down from the wall upstairs and, one by one, the incoming president, vice-president and treasurer touched the Charter as they pledged on their sacred honour to uphold the Constitution of the International Union of Mine, Mill and Smelter Workers and its duly Chartered Local Union Number 598. The oath was nearly as ancient, and certainly as solemn, as the words that Spike had read at Ben McCool's funeral, harking back to the earliest days of the old Western Fed, in the early 1890s.

The ceremony, such as it was, was conducted on the elevated stage in the mostly deserted auditorium of the Mine Mill Hall. But a photographer was present to capture a black-and-white image of the historic scene. He was standing on the floor, looking up at the figures on the stage, all of whom were wearing suits and ties. The National Officer, who had just administered the binding oath, is standing behind the wooden lectern which bore the Mine Mill seal on the front and which had, for so many years, been the bully pulpit of Spike Sworski. Immediately to his left stand the insurgents newly come to power. No one is smiling. There is no hint of celebration or relief or triumph. The three newcomers stare out over the big empty room grim-faced, as if they alone can foresee the future.

26

Tightening the Screws

Jake was the first to go—even before Gilpin.

He was summoned to the new president's office the morning after the inauguration and summarily dismissed as the personal assistant to the president of Local 598. Even to Jake, who had certainly expected this particular axe to fall, it seemed cold: there was no word of thanks, no acknowledgement of his family's long history of sacrifice for or connection with the history of Local 598. No warm recollection of organizing the union, never even any sense the Local *had* been organized. His services were no longer required, Jake was told curtly, and he was out the door.

Jake fumed over it all the way home to the Valley. Although he'd never been much of a student of history, even Jake could see the irony: like all rabid anti-Communists the newly elected officials loved to accuse the Stalin-era Soviet Union of rewriting its own history to conveniently suit dogma. Yet here were these exact same critics, now in power, treating

Jake as if the past never existed, and certainly didn't matter now.

"It *is* ironic," his father agreed. "Good thing you've still got your day job. You'll get by ..."

"Yeah, I guess so," Jake, still stung by his summary dismissal, agreed half-heartedly. And it was true—he still had a good paying job yielding a rich bonus rate on top of his lucrative hourly rate. It could be worse: he could be like Foley, who would be out of a job altogether.

Gilpin was second on the new president's hit list.

He was in and out the door just as swiftly as Jake. His writing duties would be handled by someone else, he was told. Someone, Foley surmised, much more loyal to the incoming executive than himself. And that was that. The next thing he knew he was out on Regent Street, facing Queen's Athletic Field, the December cold and an uncertain future. The bum's rush if ever there was one.

The following week the new executive took a more sweeping move to consolidate its power by closing all of the Local's satellite halls in the outlying communities of Garson, Chelmsford, Creighton and Levack. Long a pet project of Sworski's, the satellites, each of which hosted its own monthly membership meetings in tandem with meetings at the central hall, made it more convenient for members in the far-flung outlying communities to participate in the affairs of the big Local without having to travel into town.

Billed as a cost-cutting measure, the change reduced overhead and labour costs, it was true, but it also allowed for much greater control of decision-making at the centre, a power that was now carefully exercised and controlled by the new executive. Attendance at the monthly membership meetings—held in the evening and in the morning to accommodate shift workers—now became a matter of the utmost concern. The composition of many committees critical to the big Local's management—the Elections Committee, delegations to conventions—was decided by a show of hands from the floor. The Local remained highly polarized even after Sworski's ouster, and so were the membership meetings. The new executive took pains to "outpack" its rival faction at every membership meeting, even if it meant promising free beer to sympathetic attendees, or a coveted spot on a junket as a member of an official convention delegation. Sworski himself stubbornly refused to resort to such blandishments, which he considered underhanded at best, unethical at worst. As a result his supporters found themselves repeatedly outnumbered and outvoted at membership meetings. The upshot was defeatism, and a steady decline in member turnout, along with a consolidation of unchallenged power in the hands of the new executive. It was the beginning of a take-no-prisoners ethos in the Mine Mill Hall that would set the tone in union politics for decades to come: your slate would win power, riding the tiger of the Sudbury rank and file for a term or two, only to be eaten by that tiger when a new contract failed to meet expectations, or when strike leadership faltered and lost its nerve. Then your slate would be swept from office wholesale; there would be no survivors after the new slate had finished purging the executive ranks. It was a revolving-door leadership that boded poorly for any sense of continuity or collegiality within the leadership ranks of the big Local.

This decline into dysfunction was almost imperceptible at first, although it would, in hindsight, long outlast the end of the Cold War which had engendered it. The advent of slate politics in the big Local, and with it the winner-take-all ethos that fostered both cronyism and favouritism, would become the norm for later generations of leaders who had long since forgotten what had engendered the system in the first place.

This legacy of the raids infested even the workplace itself, as Jake discovered on a shift shortly after the elections.

Always a man of few words, Bob Jesperson seemed even more subdued than usual, even bordering at times on the downright surly.

Finally Jake became so irritated at his partner's uncharacteristic pouting that he broke down and asked Bob if he was all right as they were repositioning the jumbo.

"Oh yeah, I'm okay," Jesperson smiled wanly. "Lost my badge, is all ..."

"Your badge?" It took Jake a minute to process this information. "Oh, your steward's badge! How did that happen?"

Jesperson shrugged. "Oh, new president called me in, told me I was being replaced."

"Replaced! By who?"

"Harry Hoople, from what I hear."

"Hoople! But that's ridiculous!" And more than a little worrisome, Jake realized. His old nemesis, who was now in tight with the Union Hall, had gained considerable sway over Jake's well-being in the workplace. A front-line shop steward decided which grievances to prosecute, and how aggressively. If Jake were ever fired, it would be up to Hoople to fight to get his job back. Such an event seemed unlikely at the moment, but all it took was one shift boss with an agenda, or a change in shifters, and the arrival of a real asshole who just didn't like Jake's face, or who'd had a run-in with Big Bill or his Uncle Walt or his Uncle Bud before Jake was even born and who was still looking for payback these many years later. He'd have to watch his step now more than ever, Jake realized as Bob's news sank in.

"How many other stewards did he shitcan?"

Bob shrugged again, disconsolately. "I dunno. But from what I hear, he's shakin' up the whole stewards' body."

"Hmm, no shit. Now why ain't I surprised?"

As they both knew the stewards' body was the sinews—in many ways the heart and soul—of the big Local. Shop stewards policed the Collective Agreement in the workplace. Any industrial union worth its salt was only as good as its stewards' body.

Quite apart from the tightening of the screws by the new executive, work proceeded apace for Jake and his partner in their heading in the Middle Country of Frood Mine.

The trial of the new jumbo drill was proving to be an all-out success, as even Jake had to admit.

A steady stream of Frood miners passed through the heading weekly, curious to see the new contraption in operation. Reactions varied widely. Widespread doubts were expressed, especially about the floodlights attached to the jumbo.

"They're too bright—too much glare," complained one of the old guys. "I wouldn't be able to see what I was doing."

Only later did the full absurdity of the remark entirely sink in with Jake. The oldtimer had toiled in utter darkness for so long that he had, in some weird way, adapted to living without that foremost of human senses, eye-sight. The remark was some kind of backhanded tribute to the adaptability of the human species, Jake reflected, even as it demonstrated the natural tendency to resist all change.

But there were times when the jumbo had its drawbacks, especially when a drill steel became "stuck" in the breast. The same thing happened with a jackleg, of course, but the solution was more straightforward: grab for the heaviest hammer you could find and whale away on the protruding end of the steel. Give it a few shots, then get the longest-handled wrench available, and reef clockwise on it with all your might until the steel loosened up. But with the jumbo, it all seemed so much harder—Jake never understood exactly why.

Of course there were three drills turning at once, instead of just one, so the chances of one getting stuck were that much greater. Or maybe the jumbo turned with more torque, and so buried the steel that much deeper.

Breakdowns were a headache, too. The jumbos were a much more sophisticated device than the old jacklegs, with many more moving parts, and so that much more prone to break down. There wasn't much on a jackleg the old guys couldn't fix themselves in a pinch. But the jumbo, with its complex hydraulics—a new form of motive power, basically oil under immense pressure—was beyond the ken of the average miner.

And so began a subtle tilt in skill sets underground. The days of the self-reliant miner repairing his own machinery right in the stope or drift began to wane, and the number of highly skilled underground mechanics began to proliferate. Instead of bashing or patching your own jackleg into submission, you "walked" your jumbo into the nearest underground service bay, and their numbers were beginning to proliferate, too.

All of this was lost on most of the old guys who drifted into the heading to stand speechless before this marvel of modern technology, with its maze of hoses, fearsome roar, and dazzling floodlights.

"How much one 'a these set the company back?" one of them asked Bob as the drills fell silent while they repositioned the machine.

"Oh, 'bout a quarter million, I'm told," came the reply.

Only stunned silence greeted the rejoinder. Now this *was* serious business.

27

Job Interview

"I'm afraid you're damaged goods then, my friend..."

Foley Gilpin's heart sank even as the scratchy words arrived over the static of the long distance telephone line.

The speaker was Mike O'Neill, Ontario desk editor of the *Globe and Mail*, where Foley had just pitched his services on a cold, totally shot-in-the-dark call early in the New Year of 1964, a changing of the calendar he'd hoped would bring him luck in ushering in this abrupt, desperately needed career change.

He'd found O'Neill brusque, abrupt, and short of time; pretty much par for the course for any editor at any major metropolitan daily. O'Neill had wasted no time grilling Gilpin: had he worked for either of the big mining companies in Sudbury, taken money from them for doing PR?

"No."

What about the Mine Mill Union?

Here Foley was forced to pause, a moment of crackling long distance silence that did not go unnoticed, even in the clamour of the *Globe's* newsroom. He was tempted, momentarily, to lie. But the risk of exposure by the new Mine Mill in-crowd was too great. Yes, Foley confessed, he *had* done some freelance work for the union.

And then came the "damaged goods" comment.

"Oh. Well then, I'm sorry. Thanks for your time, anyway."

"Unless …"

"Yes?" Foley could sense the door opening just a crack.

"Unless we took the time to debastardize you—it would mean a few months of assignments unrelated to mining up there. Small stories mostly, just to see how you'd work out …"

"Sure," Foley assented quickly, eager to get his foot in that door that had been left, ever so slightly, ajar.

It would take years for Foley to fully appreciate that, as much as he needed an income, O'Neill was, if anything, just as eager not to lose this fish on the line—Sudbury was, after all, a sizeable northern metropolis where the *Globe* badly needed cover, and experienced reporters with Gilpin's *bona fides* did not pop up every day up there.

O'Neill was careful to ask Foley's phone number before the conversation ended, and the matter was left entirely in the air.

Or so it seemed to Foley until O'Neill himself called with an assignment a few weeks later. It wasn't much—a court case involving a large, state-owned French oil company that was being sentenced in Sudbury District Court on charges of price-fixing. After accepting the assignment with alacrity Gilpin asked about his deadline.

"Oh, better make it six p.m. … to make the bulldog." O'Neill rasped.

Gilpin scanned the courtroom, to see if any of the city's local newsrooms were represented, but he discovered to his surprise that he had the story all to himself. That, coupled with the realization that someone in the *Globe*'s newsroom three hundred miles to the south had been aware of a newsworthy event that had escaped the notice of every local editor and reporter, made a definite impression on Foley: the big Toronto daily was playing on a whole different level than the local Sudbury news media.

Foley gave the story what he thought it was worth, filing only four brief paragraphs over the phone to a rewrite man in Toronto.

He eagerly scanned the paper the next morning to learn the fate of his story—the bulldog, or early edition, was the one trucked into town, making the four-hour highway trip to Sudbury overnight. He found it buried deep inside the front news section. His four 'graphs had been chopped back to two—the top two. But, Foley noted with quiet satisfaction, those two paragraphs were, word for word, exactly what he had written.

The pattern was repeated a few times over the next nine months until, Foley hoped, he had been sufficiently 'debastardized.' As a test, he pitched O'Neill what he considered would be the biggest breaking national news story Sudbury had produced during his freelance tenure: Local 598's membership meeting the next night was expected to deliberate suspending its dues check-off to the Mine Mill National Office. If the insurgent-led move carried, Gilpin explained, it would be a major body-blow to Mine Mill's Canadian wing, perhaps even resulting in its collapse—the financial support of the big Sudbury Local was that large a part of the national organization's overall budget. And the demise of such an historic, reputedly Communist-led labour organization would be an event of clearly national significance.

Silence greeted his pitch as O'Neill weighed the angles, but there was no mistaking the *Globe* editor's interest. This time, Foley sensed, it was *he* who had the big fish on the line. Foley paused. He *wanted* this story, wanted to be in the Mine Mill Hall on this historic night.

Finally, he could hear O'Neill drawing a deep breath. "All right, Gilpin, I'll take it ... But if you fuck this up, it'll mean my ass first, and then yours second. Got that?"

Foley's heart leapt at the response, but he was careful to conceal his elation.

"Right. Sure."

Monthly membership meetings of Sudbury's big mining locals are, to this very day, routinely closed to reporters, and this one was no exception. As a result, Gilpin found himself cooling his heels in the Hall lobby outside the heavy wooden doors that concealed the union's business from the handful of reporters waiting outside. Already, Foley sensed, his presence was noticed by his colleagues. It meant *The Globe and Mail* was interested in a story, which in itself lent an event greater significance.

Feeling more than slightly foolish, Foley took his turn attempting to peer through the gap between the doors, which were joined tightly enough that not even the slightest tantalizing glimpse was possible. And the doors themselves were solid enough to muffle all sound.

How times had changed! Where, only a few months before, he had enjoyed unquestioned admission to the Union's executive offices and its innermost thoughts, now here he was on the outside looking in. He might be 'debastardized' in the newsroom of *The Globe and Mail*, Gilpin reflected, but he was now an outlying bastard in the Mine Mill Hall.

Suddenly Gilpin felt a heavy hand on his shoulder, jerking on him, spinning him around. Before he could quite come to his senses the newsman found himself pushed back to the wall on the far side of the lobby, breathing the sour whiskey breath and seeing—in far too close a detail—the chin stubble of some union bully boy he'd never met before, but who seemed about to take a poke at him.

"Git away from that door, you cock-sucking Commie stooge!"

The pudgy little newspaperman, his glasses askew on his nose, was clearly terrified at this sudden assault and he was staring in disbelief into a snarling, gap-toothed face when, suddenly, it was gone.

"Hoople, you asshole, when you gonna start picking on somebody your own size?" Gilpin recognized the voice of Jake McCool, who had grabbed his assailant by the shoulder and spun him around. Behind Jake, and clearly spoiling for a fight, stood three older men, as tall as Jake, but much stockier.

Hoople sized up the four of them, and didn't much like his odds.

"McCool!" he sputtered. He jerked loose, out of Jake's grasp, and stalked off across the lobby, shaking a fist back at Jake. "Anytime, buddy, anytime! And I just hope you never need a steward on the job!"

Foley struggled to catch his breath. "Jake! Am I ever glad to see you!"

Jake, clearly in his element, shot the newsman a reassuring grin. "You okay, Foley?" And then he lowered his voice. "You wait right here. I'll tell ya what happens inside soon's I come out."

Foley could only nod in mute gratitude.

28

Déjà Vu All Over Again

Jake strode across the lobby and pounded hard on the wooden doors, which were opened a crack by the Sergeant-at-Arms, who looked Hoople and the McCools up and down, nodded, and swung the double doors open wide.

The scene inside was all very familiar to Jake. The meeting was already under way, the same old tension, the air thick, blue with cigarette smoke, funky with the smell of sweat. The same wide aisle ran down the centre of the big Hall, splitting the rank and file into two seated groups. But now the seating order had reversed, with Hoople peeling off to sit with his comrades on the left, and the McCools pulling up chairs on the right. Their group, Jake couldn't help noticing, was now visibly smaller than the one across the aisle—not even close. The faces at the long table up on the stage had also changed completely, of course, but the antipathy between the two groups down on the floor remained, as evident as ever.

Jake studied his union brothers as the speeches droned on. They were a nondescript bunch—old guys, mainly—dressed in workers' garb—baggy, dark blue pants over matching shirts, or the same outfits, almost uniforms, really, in dark green. A rough, foul-mouthed, hard-drinking, hard-working crowd, at home in a workshop or in the bush. Stubborn, self-reliant and resilient men who were functionally illiterate in both of Canada's official languages because they had been forced to drop out of school at an early age in the Dirty Thirties, first to work on the farm, then to march off to fight Hitler.

Finally it was time for the main event—the moment they'd all been waiting for.

"And so I move, Mister Chairman, that in light of the total lack of support for this Local Union in our darkest hour of need—the fact that we received no strike pay from the National Office—after we poured good money into that organization for years—and where did our money go, Mister Chairman? ... And so I move that we discontinue our check-off payments to this do-nothing buncha bastards, effective immediately!"

The crowd across the aisle, swept up in this peroration, roared its approval.

The new president gavelled for order and accepted the motion.

"And the Chair recognizes the Brother over there." He was pointing at Sworski, who was sitting at the front of Jake's group.

Spike, about the only rank-and-filer wearing a suit and tie, spoke passionately, even eloquently, against the motion. He proposed a series of manoeuvres to delay or defer the action, each of which was put to a vote, and each of which was quickly defeated by a show of hands from the floor, each side voting as a solid bloc—and Spike's bloc was clearly a minority, reduced now to a sorry and ever diminishing rump.

Finally, inexorably, the main motion was put to a vote. The unspoken purpose, as, to a man, the multitude well understood, was to drive a dagger through the heart of the Canadian wing of the Mine Mill Union.

And it passed, with a great roar of approval and the thunderous stomping of work boots on the hollow-sounding wooden floor. *This is the way the world ends, this is the way the world ends.*

All around him Jake could practically see the shoulders sag, the air come out of the balloon, as one by one Sworski's adherents quietly made for the exits. Even the last remnant of his small rump was melting away.

Jake joined the quiet exodus, found Gilpin waiting anxiously just outside the doors.

"Well?"

Jake shook his head grimly. "It passed."

Outwardly, at least, Gilpin greeted this news with equanimity, but inwardly his feelings were decidedly mixed. On the one hand his story had panned out, which was good for his career—and his pocketbook. On the other, he felt sorry for his old friend Sworski, and for the demise of the scrappy old union he was almost certainly bearing witness to.

"Wanna join us for a beer downstairs?" Jake asked Gilpin, motioning at the three large men who were still behind him.

"Sure. You bet."

They trooped down to the union tap room, where their entrance did not pass unnoticed. They were greeted by hard stares of unmitigated hostility, which Foley, after his recent encounter with Hoople, found unnerving. But the McCools seemed oblivious to the cold shoulder. Soon Foley had met Jake's father and uncles, and he'd reached into the pocket of his trench coat for his pen and notebook.

"So, what happened up there?"

Jake just sighed and shook his head, and his elders looked equally bereft.

"We got our clocks cleaned," Jake answered quietly.

"They think they've killed the Mine Mill Union," one of the senior McCools said softly—Gilpin thought it was Bud, but he wasn't sure—he *hated* these group interviews. "Down, but not out, is what I say." He wrapped a big mitt around his draft glass. "Here's to the Mine Mill!"

His brothers and nephew quickly raised their own glasses, tapping the rims softly together, and Foley joined in.

"But what actually *happened?*" Gilpin pressed.

"We got outvoted," Jake shrugged.

"Oh yeah we did," agreed Jake's dad, suppressing a snort of indignation.

"But ya gotta hand it to 'em," one of the uncles said ruefully. "They sure know how to pack a meeting."

"Christ, yes," agreed the other uncle. "Ever notice how we seem to be the only ones actually *paying* for our drinks?"

"But it gets results, Uncle Walt," Jake remonstrated.

"Aye, laddy," Walt McCool agreed. "And it *is* a form of organizing, I suppose."

Bill McCool grunted and surveyed the room with a baleful glare. "If you can call *this* organized."

Gilpin felt increasingly apprehensive, sensing that the despairing mood at the table was on the edge of boiling over into dark, menacing rage. He had a story to write.

Even now the words of his lede were circling inside his head like some spinning carousel. He knew from long experience it wouldn't stop until he got them tamed, ordered and written down.

Gilpin rose, shrugged into his trench coat, and excused himself, muttering an explanation about having a story to write.

Of course his story wasn't due until six o'clock of the following evening, so Foley took his time to get it right. This would be the first news feature he'd filed to the *Globe,* and by far the most substantial piece of writing. He'd even managed to find a Labour History prof out in B.C. who was willing to predict on the record that the loss of Local 598's hefty dues payments would likely lead to the demise of the Mine Mill in Canada—the prof was the type of source known as "a pipe-puffer" in the business. Gilpin balanced him out with the "down but not out" quote he'd picked up from whichever of the McCool elders in the bar the night before. He attributed that to "a veteran union insider."

Gilpin wrote the story as he always did—on the same portable typewriter he'd carted from Chicago to Guatemala City and back to Chicago and on to D.C. before moving back to Chicago one last time and then on to Canada. He typed it out double spaced to leave room for edits—of which there were many— before he finally picked up the phone to dictate the finished product to the rewrite men in Toronto. It had, as Gilpin knew, all the elements of any great news story: bitter infighting and a struggle to the death for power, rich history and colourful local lore, and, perhaps the death throes of a legendary trade union whose roots ran deep—all the way back to the turn of the last century—a history Gilpin summarized as succinctly as he could. In the end it ran to nearly three "takes," or pages, and, after countless edits Gilpin was well pleased with the result.

The next morning he scanned the *Globe* bulldog more eagerly than usual. He was delighted to find his story on page three. Not the front page—which had been described as "the most influential newspaper real estate in Canada" because of the way it set the day's national news agenda in newsrooms across the city of Toronto—but page three was the next best thing. Still no by-line, either, Gilpin noticed, even though it was longer and more prominently displayed than many of the staffers' stories which did run under by-lines, but Mike O'Neill was notoriously stingy with by-lines when it came to his stringers, of which he had a legion. Foley, in fact, had never had a by-line in *The Globe and Mail*. No matter—the story had received the best play he'd had yet, which told him that, by-line or no, his work was being noticed—and appreciated—by someone in the nether regions of the paper's editorial management. A big fish had risen to the bait, and now, Foley sensed, he was about to set the hook.

Provincial Courthouse (Oryst Sawchuk)

29

Spike's Plants Come Home to Roost

The morning's *Globe*, carefully folded to Gilpin's story, made its way around the big oak table before coming to rest where it had started—in front of the national president of the Canadian Union of the Mine, Mill and Smelter Workers' Union, who was chairing this emergency meeting of his executive board.

He tapped on the paper. "So, what do we do now?"

The story had not caught his National Executive Board entirely by surprise—Spike Sworski had forewarned them such a move was in the offing. Even still, the mood around the table was sombre.

"Trusteeship!" came the first response.

The president grunted noncommittally. He had expected this knee-jerk response from an especially hawkish member of his board.

"Anyone else?" He scanned each of the faces turned towards him up and down the long boardroom table.

Only silence and a stubborn, gloomy air greeted his query.

He paused reflectively. Trusteeship—where the national executive appointed a trustee to run a Local's affairs, effectively revoking its charter, was a legal and time-honoured means of dealing with a rogue Local whose executive members were guilty of financial malfeasance or violating the Union's Constitution. But trusteeship was a draconian, last-resort measure, and this situation was different—far more delicate. The new executive up in Sudbury had been duly elected, after all, by a rank and file that everyone around the table knew, and respected. How would such a heavy-handed response play out with Sudbury's hard-nosed, volatile rank and file?

"It's risky," the president said at last. Several heads around the table bobbed in agreement.

"So is doing nothing!" insisted the outspoken, hard-line board member.

Once again the president noted heads nodding in agreement. The board numbers appeared to be about evenly divided. Where no one dissented was that something must be done—their backs really were against the wall; inaction was not an option.

And so the debate was joined.

"Abe, what can you tell us?" the president directed his question at Abraham Bluestein, the union's Toronto legal counsel.

Bluestein cleared his throat, and began speaking carefully, as he always did.

"Well, first of all, trusteeship is certainly a viable legal option in this case. But politically, the issue may not be so clear cut. If the ultimate concern here is not to lose the hearts and minds—to say nothing of the dues dollars—of the members of Local 598, then an overly hasty move to trusteeship could present an untenable risk over the long term ..." The lawyer paused to let his words sink in.

Silence greeted his equivocating observations.

"What about the assets, Abe?" asked the national treasurer, breaking the silence at last.

"The bricks and mortar, the properties up there, yes," Bluestein nodded. "Excellent question. I suppose a *prima facie* case could easily be made that all of that, which was paid for by the members of the Mine Mill Union, remains the property of the Mine Mill Union; most courts are inclined to regard such property rights as inviolable and applicable in perpetuity ..."

The president paused reflectively, before posing another question. "So if we could prove that the new executive up there was conspiring to confiscate our property illegally, and to transfer ownership to another entity—say, another union—would that provide legal grounds for an injunction to oust that new executive, give them the old heave-ho off our property?"

"Ye-es, I suppose the answer would be yes," replied Bluestein. He looked down the table at the president. "But have you such evidence?"

The president paused, and looked down at the table, stumped.

"No, I suppose not, Abe," he admitted reluctantly at last.

The debate droned on through the lunch hour, until, finally, in mid-afternoon, the group reached a consensus: Local 598 would be placed in trusteeship, after all. The national vice-president, a mild-mannered and unassuming individual, would be dispatched to Sudbury to "babysit" the new local executive and to serve as trustee. Abraham Bluestein would accompany him in the event that the opportunity for legal action might present itself.

They arrived at the Junction, an obscure, little-used whistle stop in the farthest northeast reaches of central Sudbury. This was standard practice for Mine Mill officials wanting to come and go while avoiding the myriad of prying eyes likely to be present at the city's bustling downtown passenger railway depot on Elgin Street.

Abe Bluestein felt as he always did whenever he ventured up to the northern mining capital; the place struck him as raw, uncivilized. It still felt like a frontier town: wild, uncouth, even a little dangerous. The whole scene struck him as starkly surreal as he stepped down onto the platform of the Sudbury Junction.

Their train pulled out of the station—little more than a shack, really—almost as soon as they had stepped off, and Bluestein and his companion were left alone to find their bearings in the black expanse of the limitless bush that surrounded Sudbury.

For the first time in his life, Bluestein, who had made a career out of representing progressive, left-wing clients, felt he truly was an agent in the Cold War. There was a clandestinity in the darkness and isolation of this arrival.

A single streetlight illuminated the scene, throwing sharp, angular shadows that reminded Bluestein of old Bogart movies. Right on cue a tall figure in a trench coat emerged from the shadows beneath the eaves of the shack cum station. His face was obscured by the brim of a snap-brim fedora pulled low on his head.

"Welcome to Sudbury, gentlemen." The voice was low, but warm and familiar.

"Spike? Are we ever glad to see *you!*" Bluestein pumped Sworski's outstretched hand.

They briefed Sworski on the national office decision as he drove them through the eastern outskirts of the city to his home in Coniston.

"How do you think it'll play, Spike?"

"What, the trusteeship, you mean? That all depends. The new executive'll hate it, that's for sure. The membership'll be split right down the middle. Personally, I'm all for it."

Spike pulled up into his driveway. "C'mon in. I'll make us a pot of fresh coffee."

The trio had just settled into Sworski's house, and were sipping at their coffees around the kitchen table when there was a loud rapping at the door.

There was something about the urgency of the loud, rapping staccato knocks that startled all three of them.

"Were you expecting someone?" Bluestein asked Sworski.

"What? At this hour? No, not at all," Spike replied as he rushed to the door.

He glanced through the window in the door before quickly swinging it open.

A big, shambling bear of a man stood at the kitchen door.

"Brother Alaavo!" Spike exclaimed, clearly surprised. "Come in, come in! What brings you out at such an hour?"

"Sorry it's so late, Spike, but I seen your lights was on, I'm just back from Sturgeon, and I thought you'd want to know what just happened—Oh, I'm sorry, didn't mean to interrupt—"

"No, no, it's quite all right, Risto. Here, let me introduce you. Whatever you have to tell me you can say to these gentlemen …"

Spike went on to explain to Bluestein and his other guest that Risto Alaavo, a Coniston smelterman also known as "Grizzly," had, since the previous summer, been one of a pair of trusted Mine Mill veterans he'd assigned to the special duty of "shadowing" the leaders of the insurgency within the Local. They had been instructed to work closely with the insurgents, to win their trust over time and to report personally to Spike.

"So, what was going on in Sturgeon River, Ted?" Spike asked as he poured the big man a coffee.

"Special meetin'. Listen to who all was there—" He rhymed off names that were familiar to everyone at the table. Beside the newly elected president, vice-president and recording secretary of Local 598, Alaavo listed a well-known CCF Member of Parliament, the vice-president of the Canadian Congress of Labour, and the senior Canadian man in the United Steelworkers of America. "And they were talkin' about Steel takin' over the Local! Just like that! I couldn't friggin' believe it!"

Spike nodded, and shot a glance at his guests. Bluestein was already on the move, towards his coat, which was hanging beside the door. "If you don't mind, Mister—ah—Alaavo, is it? I'll just write some of this down if you don't mind ..." The lawyer fished a pen and notepad out of his coat pocket.

Alaavo looked at Sworski, who nodded reassuringly.

"No, sir, no problem at all, you go right ahead," the big man replied.

Bluestein returned to the table and sat down. "Now who exactly did you say was at this meeting?"

The nocturnal visitor repeated his story, which left no doubt that a conspiracy was already afoot to turn Local 598 into a Steel affiliate.

Bluestein nodded his head, scribbling as fast as he could. Spike and the national vice-president peppered Alaavo with a few clarifying questions, and then thanked him. Solski ushered Alaavo to the door, and returned to the table. The trio exchanged glances of disbelief at this sudden turn of events.

Bluestein shook his head. Hard to believe, the boldness of it all! But that was Sudbury. Raw, big-shouldered, in-your-face Sudbury.

Sworski glanced at the lawyer, could practically see the wheels turning. "So, Abe, where does this leave us?"

Bluestein suppressed a chuckle. "Well, it's the very evidence we were looking for that would allow us to file for an *ex parte* injunction from the court declaring that the Hall and all the other properties up here are still the property of the Union of the Mine, Mill and Smelter Workers.

"I'll dictate this," he tapped his notepad, "to one of the girls in the office in the morning, get her to type it up, get Mr. Alaavo back into the Hall to review and sign his deposition, get him to swear to it before me, as a Commissioner of Oaths, and we'll have an affidavit that should be admissible as evidence in a court of law ..."

"So in the morning," Sworski spoke first to the vice-president before turning to Bluestein, relishing the words, "you turn up to relieve the executive of their duties, while *you*," he turned to Bluestein, "go into court to have them evicted!"

"Anyone for more coffee?"

Sworski's blueprint unfolded according to plan the next day—the new executive was caught completely off guard by the trusteeship, while Abe Bluestein's labours on the Alaavo affidavit were also completed. The Toronto lawyer even found time for a quick call to his Sudbury counterpart, Leonard Pharand, who often acted on Local 598's behalf on the more frequent, minor matters when the national office opted to forego Bluestein's hefty hourly fee in favour of more local, and less expensive, legal representation. Pharand agreed to appear when Bluestein filed his *ex parte* application the next day.

Bluestein, who had never set foot in the Sudbury courthouse, was relieved to have a local colleague in his corner. The pair had agreed to meet "at the docket," the roadmap, posted daily, to the day's proceedings in a highly visible location in every Canadian courthouse. But even there Bluestein was at a loss, and forced to ask directions in the swirl of activity as solicitors, in their long, black flowing robes, and their sketchy-looking, twitchy clientele, arrived to begin another day that would determine the fate of dozens of accused, and that would conclude with many of them sitting behind bars.

Abe Bluestein was relieved to find Len Pharand at last, peering over the docket. He turned to Bluestein on the broad grin with a look of wonder on his face.

"We're in Courtroom A." And then, in a whisper *"You must have a horseshoe up your ass, Abe. You drew Judge Carson!"*

The name meant nothing to the Toronto lawyer.

"Judge Otto Kearns Carson!" Pharand explained, still in a whisper. *"'Okay' Carson! He's known as Judge 'Okay' Carson because he's never been known to deny a motion!* Well, hardly ever, anyway. Here, follow me."

Courtroom A was the most spacious, and by far the most formal, courtroom in the Sudbury courthouse, as Bluestein could see. High-ceilinged and trimmed in handsome hardwood, the room was illuminated principally by the abundant natural light that streamed in through stately windows that lined the west wall of the big room.

Most of Courtroom A was furnished with rows of dark wooden seats, which reminded Bluestein of the pews at Synagogue, or, he supposed, inside a Christian church. The courtroom was beginning to fill up with burly, awkward men—clearly uncertain about being in a courtroom. Some wore Mine Mill jackets, others Steelworkers' parkas.

A low railing separated the spectators from the Court's active participants. Bluestein and Pharand took their place at the Plaintiff's table, which was at the front of the room, directly beneath the bench. The Defendant's table was vacant. Bluestein's surprise legal manoeuvre, much less his presence, had apparently caught the Steelworkers' legal team unawares. Bluestein frowned at this development. Any conscientious judge might adjourn the proceeding forthwith as a fundamental violation of due process—with only one side represented.

At that moment the Clerk called the Court to order, ushering Judge Carson into the room. Everyone rose as Carson climbed onto the bench. Bluestein studied him closely. Carson was an older man, his stocky build and ample girth evident even beneath his all-concealing judicial robes. His balding head was ringed by a retreating fringe of dark brown hair. Not the sort of man to stand out in a crowd. Not the sort of man, Bluestein judged, who would be much of anything stripped of the awe-inspiring trappings of office—the judge's robes, the quaint wing-collared white shirt, the commanding heights of the judicial dais. But, even still, Bluestein caught Carson's eyes surveying his domain, noting at once the empty table where the counsel for the defendants should have been.

To Bluestein's relief, Carson gavelled his court to order nevertheless.

Carson cleared his throat and studied a sheaf of papers that had been laid out for him by the Clerk. "So, what have we here, Mister—Mister?" He looked uncertainly down at Bluestein and Pharand.

Abe jumped quickly to his feet. "Abraham Bluestein for the plaintiffs, your Honour, along with my co-counsel, Leonard Pharand. We're here this morning to seek an *ex parte* injunction declaring the Mine Mill Hall, 198 Regent Street, Sudbury to be solely the property of the Canadian Division of the International Union of Mine, Mill and Smelter Workers' Union, in fee simple, with all the usual privileges and rights that attach thereto ..."

"I see, I see ..." Carson nodded gravely. "But are these rights in any way in jeopardy, Mr.—ah, Mr. Bluestein?"

"Yes, we believe that they are, your Honour. As you are doubtless aware, sir, the property in question, as well as several other ancillary properties throughout the Sudbury District as enumerated in our application, have been purchased over the years by the Mine Mill Union through the accrual of dues lawfully paid by the members of Local 598 to the union. But we now have reason to believe that the newly elected executive board members of Local 598 are engaged in an active, *sub rosa* conspiracy to alienate these properties from their rightful owners."

"But these executive board officers have only just been democratically elected, have they not, Mr. Bluestein? This court is normally loathe to interfere in the internal affairs of any legal, democratically run organization. Have you any evidence to adduce to prove the existence of this alleged conspiracy, as you call it?"

"We have, your Honour." Bluestein nodded to Pharand, who rose to deliver the Alaavo affidavit to the Clerk. "If it please the Court I now enter the sworn affidavit of one Risto Alaavo, as taken by me, and dated just yesterday, in the Judicial District of Sudbury. If it please the Court, we would enter this as Plaintiffs' Exhibit A, your Honour."

Carson quickly scrutinized the document, which had been handed up to him by the Clerk. "I see, I see … and is the deponent here in this Court?"

"He is, your Honour." Bluestein nodded, bowing slightly at the waist. He turned to the rows of benches behind him, caught Alaavo's eye, and motioned for him to come forward.

The burly smelterman, clearly out of his element, shambled through the gate in the low railing into the well of the Court where he was duly sworn to tell the truth, the whole truth and nothing but the truth before entering the witness box.

"Now, Mr. Alaavo I have just a few questions for you." Carson lowered his voice genially, apparently out of deference to Alaavo's uneasiness with his unfamiliar surroundings.

To Bluestein's pleasure, Alaavo turned out to be an excellent witness, answering most questions with a simple "yes" or "no" while refraining from any tendency to fence with the Judge.

It was unusual, but not unheard of, for a Judge to cross-examine a witness from the bench. The absence of counsel for the defence made the practice all the more acceptable to Bluestein, who witnessed Judge Carson's cross of Alaavo with mounting admiration for Spike's informant. Outwardly, however, Bluestein remained absolutely deadpan as he watched his only witness in the box. But Alaavo kept shifting his weight from one foot to another—the result of his nervousness at this entire affair, Abe realized. Alaavo's constant swaying bothered him nonetheless.

Carson drew from Alaavo a detailed repetition of the meeting he'd attended a few days earlier in Sturgeon River.

"And how was it you came to be at this meeting in the first place, Mr. Alaavo?"

The big man hesitated, and looked down at the floor, blushing slightly. "Well, sir, Mister Sworski asked me last summer, sir, to work close to these fellers, stay close to 'em, kinda like …"

"So you were spying on them?" Carson observed mildly.

"Well, yes, sir, I guess you could say that," Alaavo conceded, blushing still more deeply.

"Very well, then, Mr. Alaavo, I have no more questions. You may step down, sir."

The case for the Plaintiff was now complete, and, in the absence of counsel for the defence, the matter was now concluded.

Bluestein fully expected Carson to reserve his decision, but what happened next came as a complete surprise.

"I'd like to thank counsel for the plaintiff for making its case with such speed," Carson intoned. "The Court is prepared to render judgment in this matter shortly. I now declare a fifteen minute recess." Carson rapped his wooden gavel on the bench sharply.

Bluestein looked at Pharand in surprise. "This is how he works," the Sudbury lawyer shrugged, once again with a broad grin. The two lawyers left the Courtroom to have a quick smoke out in the hallway. They had barely finished their cigarettes when the Clerk approached them. "He's back!" he announced. Carson was still settling into his chair as they re-entered the Courtroom, after pausing at the doorway to offer the customary bow from the waist.

Carson looked down at them from his throne-like perch, and gravely cleared his throat before beginning to speak.

"Gentlemen, I have given this matter careful consideration, and it does appear that the Plaintiffs have met the onus as required by the Statute. Since a *prima facie* case has been established, I do hereby grant the requested *ex parte* remedy, as requested by the Plaintiffs."

"Yes!" exulted Bluestein, who suppressed his strong impulse to yell out the word and pump the air with his fist. Instead, he turned calmly to Pharand and smiled, offering his hand. Bluestein was so excited he was barely conscious of a rustle, a movement, in the spectators' bench behind him.

Abraham Bluestein declined Pharand's offer of a lift back to the Mine Mill Hall, opting instead to walk the two city blocks from the courthouse up the Elm Street hill to the Union Hall. He wanted to be alone to savour this moment, and to let the fresh spring air fill his lungs and clear his head during the brisk uphill walk. He drank in the irony of the moment along with the refreshing air: how many times had he lost defences against the same legal manoeuvre he had just used? The *ex parte* injunction was a standard legal weapon, usually wielded by the employing class against organized labour, and usually granted with the same alacrity as that just displayed by the aptly nicknamed Honourable Mr. Justice 'Okay' Carson. It was routinely invoked any time employers wanted to clamp down on the number of strikers allowed to picket outside their plant gates, or to clear out a messy plant occupation. In Canada, Bluestein had long since come to realize, "the rule of law" meant first and foremost the protection of private property, the careful preservation and guardianship of the power and privilege enjoyed by the wealthy few who sat atop the commanding heights of the national economy. And now, the totally unexpected—and, for Abraham Bluestein, the unprecedented—day had finally come when he was able to wield the ruling class's own weapon against it on behalf of a union client! Brilliant! The flukiness of it—his luck in drawing 'Okay' Carson to hear his case in the first place—was all but forgotten as the Toronto lawyer reached the corner of Elm and Regent. So deep in thought was he that Abraham Bluestein was almost oblivious to the steady mid-afternoon exodus that was taking place as he neared the Mine Mill Hall.

Big Bill and Jake McCool were not usually the kind of men who would be found in the bar in the afternoon, but this was no ordinary afternoon. Like the old warhorse he was, the elder McCool had been drawn inexorably into town, into the Union Hall, to await news of the outcome of the court case being held at the courthouse just down the hill. Before he'd left home he called Frood Mine to get word to his son to join him for a drink after shift at the Mine Mill Hall, on the off chance there might be reason to celebrate. Within minutes of arriving at the Hall Big Bill learned that the newly elected executive had decamped for Port Colborne nearly at the moment the trustee arrived the day before. The port, on the shores of Lake Erie far to the south on the Niagara Peninsula, was where Inco operated a nickel refinery. It was therefore home to a small sister Local of 598, with whose executive the Sudbury leaders had travelled south to meet, at least ostensibly. There was much speculation that the trio's real destination had been Toronto, to huddle with their Steelworker masters in light of the sudden new developments in Sudbury, which had now gotten alarmingly out of control.

Big Bill and his son had just settled comfortably in to enjoy their second round when Dustin Carmody, a Levack miner and long-time Mine Mill loyalist, burst into the room. "We done it!" he announced. Carmody was still breathless from his run up the hill from the courthouse. "We won the case! We're still in the Mine Mill! Old Judge Carson himself just said so!"

Carmody's tidings ran through the cavernous tap room like an electric current. The effects, however, differed markedly from table to table in the big room. In some corners the news was greeted with jubilation, while in others it was met with stunned, sullen disbelief. Suddenly, disgruntled Steel supporters began heading for the exits, like fans leaving a sporting event early because they believed their team was doomed to lose.

Big Bill was on his feet, too, but for a different reason. He headed straight for Carmody. The portly, bespectacled Levack miner was well known to be hard of hearing, and half blind.

"Dusty!" Big Bill yelled, to get Carmody's attention. He reached out and clasped the newcomer's shoulders in both hands, as if to steady him. "It's Big Bill McCool! Exactly what did the Judge say? Settle down now, and tell us exactly what Carson said in his ruling!"

Carmody, who was still hopping from foot to foot with excitement, nodded that he understood. He breathed loudly before responding. "Well, Big Bill, what he said was this here Hall is still ours! Lock, stock and barrel! Still belongs to the Mine Mill, Big Bill, no matter what those Steel bastards says or does! And that there's the long and short of 'er, by God!"

"Okay. Dusty, all right! Thanks for bringing us the news!" McCool replied, slapping Carmody on the shoulder one more time before releasing him and returning to his table.

But the father-son bonding time was to prove short-lived. No sooner had Carmody left the room than another newcomer arrived, bearing still more news.

"Listen up, everybody!" he blared out to the room, addressing no one in particular. "There's a meetin'! Spike's called a meetin' upstairs! Startin' right away! Pitter-patter, fellas!"

One by one the tables in the taproom emptied as the members relinquished their drinks to answer Sworski's summons.

Jake looked at his father. "Guess we better go up and see what the fuss is all about," Big Bill said, rising from the table once again. And so father and son joined the general exodus, about to begin one of the most memorable nights of their lives.

As they entered the main hall Jake noticed one change right away in the cavernous meeting room: the two blocks of chairs separated by the wide central aisle had given way to a single, rectangular cluster of chairs for the rank and file. There were many fewer chairs overall, but there was now a sense of unity, almost of coziness even, that was entirely novel to Jake as he and his father slipped into their seats. Sworski was waiting up on the stage, at his accustomed post behind the old wooden podium with the venerable Mine Mill crest carved in the front. The newly ousted union president opened the meeting with a brief update of the recent developments: following the last membership meeting where the Local had voted to suspend its payments to the National Office, the National Office had decided to place Local 598 in trusteeship, and had sent the national vice-president, along with special counsel Abraham Bluestein, to Sudbury to take matters in hand on behalf of the Canadian wing of the Mine Mill Union.

It had also come to their attention that just a few days earlier a secret meeting regarding 598's future had taken place in Sturgeon River. Sworski went on to detail the attendees at the now notorious meeting, a revelation that triggered a low murmur of disbelief and anger among those surrounding Jake.

Based on this information, Sworski continued, Abe Bluestein had sought an *ex parte* injunction against the newly elected executives, enjoining them from any action that might alienate the property of the Mine Mill Union from the members of the Mine Mill. "And only moments ago, I'm happy to tell you, brothers, the Court ruled in our favour!"

Sworski was interrupted by an outburst of cheering and applause.

And nor was that all, the long-time former president added. The new executive had not taken the news of the trusteeship at all well, and they had left together in a huff, to attend to union business elsewhere, supposedly in Port Colborne. Finally Sworski paused. "Are there any questions?"

Tommy Rafftery was on his feet at once. He was seated in the front row, and he turned now to address the gathering. Everyone knew Rafftery as a hardcore Mine Miller who led the notorious "flying squad." Should an unwary Mine Miller wearing his union jacket stumble unwittingly into a Steelworker bar and find himself surrounded by hostile Steel goons, he needed only to reach a telephone and call Tommy Rafftery. Rafftery would do the rest, calling the Simard brothers and a couple of other scrappers, and within minutes they'd converge on the bar and rescue their beleaguered brother in a fine frenzy of broken glass and blood and beer. Tommy Rafftery was a Golden Gloves boxer, it was true, but during the raids he and his flying squad aimed to break bones and inflict grievous bodily harm. Their aim was not merely to hurt their victims, but to hospitalize them. What other way was there to fight back against a much larger, more powerful force from outside the community that seemed intent on destroying their much-loved, hard-won union?

Rafftery was also a hot-tempered speaker, and he gave full vent to the anger, frustration and elation they were all feeling, urging action now, direct action, to make good the Court's ruling: "This is our Union Hall!" he thundered, "and no buncha blacklegged Steelworker scabby bastards is gonna take it from us! I say we occupy the cocksucker—excuse my French—and send those gutless stooges all the way back to Pittsburgh!"

The meeting roared its approval, and a handful of Rafftery's friends vaulted suddenly onto the stage. The rest were on their feet and surging toward the stage. Rafftery's bully boys reached down to pull another half-dozen or so members up onto the stage, and, accompanied by a colossal roar from those still down below, they rushed toward the startled Sworski, and hoisted the union leader right off his feet and onto their shoulders.

Jake tensed, and found himself instinctively watching Spike's reaction to being manhandled, but Sworski's initial consternation quickly gave way to a wide smile. The union leader soon relaxed, and yielded to the myriad of rough hands who were passing him feet first overhead and down off the stage. On the floor a handful of strapping rank-and-filers were waiting to hoist Sworski triumphantly onto their shoulders. They led the assembly to the door of the Hall, stopping abruptly when they realized that the door frame was much too low to allow them to pass through with Spike borne aloft on their shoulders. They put Spike down, and Jake watched as Sworski hastily straightened his suit and tie, which had gone askew in the melee. He stepped through the door and out to the foyer, where he was once again hoisted aloft at the head of the joyous, boisterous procession. He was carried to the stairs to the second floor, and steadied himself on the shoulders of his bearers as they began to climb the broad staircase.

Jake, relaxed now that he saw Spike was in no real danger, had fallen to the back of the procession as it ascended the broad steps leading to the second floor.

At that moment Foley Gilpin arrived at the Hall. Sensing the chaos at once, he turned to Jake. "What'd I miss?" What's going on here?"

"Crazy shit!" declared Jake. "I've never seen anything like it! Looks like we're gonna occupy the Mine Mill Hall!"

But the little reporter only frowned at Jake's news. "Oh yeah? Better come look at this." He led Jake down the stairs from the foyer to the street level entrance doors to the Hall, and gestured at something outside the glassed-in doors at the entrance. Jake glanced out towards Regent Street, and there was Henry Hoople standing at the centre of a small knot of visibly angry Steelworker supporters. Jake's old nemesis appeared to be passing a flask of something around and giving orders, pointing towards downtown, dispatching a pair of his followers in that direction. Jake knew that Hoople's star had risen steadily in the union since the ascendency of the new executive and his own appointment as shop steward, and now it appeared he was taking charge of a small but determined gang of union dissidents who wanted no part of what was transpiring inside the Mine Mill Hall. With the new executive out of town, it even appeared that Hoople had become the leader of the pro-Steel faction by default. Jake turned away from the door. "Hey, Dad! Come check this out!"

Big Bill quickly descended from the now-deserted lobby to the front door. He, too, frowned as he peered through the glass door. "Hmmm. Somebody better let Spike know ..."

Father and son then hastened up the two flights of stairs, first to the lobby, then around the corner up the stairs that led to the second floor offices where they discovered the jubilant crowd had deposited Spike back onto his feet just outside his old office.

"Go in, Spike!"

"Yeah, it's where ya belong!"

Sworski appeared hesitant at first, but then he broke into a broad smile. "Very well then." He tried the door. It was unlocked, and he went right in.

The crowd cheered. Even the secretaries, who had been flustered at first by all the rough commotion, were relaxed and smiling now.

Big Bill shouldered his way through the crowd, and Jake followed. They reached Spike's office, tapped on the door, and entered swiftly. They found Sworski alone, still re-adjusting his desk chair.

"Spike, Henry Hoople's organizing his goon squad out there on the street, and I don't like the looks of it," Bill McCool warned his old friend and comrade in arms in a low voice. "This thing could get rough ... Might be a good idea to send the girls home early."

Sworski's good humour evaporated instantly, as he moved toward the window to see for himself.

Jake tensed once again. "Better be careful at that window, Spike—Mr. Sworski, sir ..."

Sworski paused briefly to look down on the knot of protesters below, which had now grown to a small band in the gathering dusk.

The union leader returned to his desk and tilted the chair back before clasping his hands in a meditative pose. Then he turned toward Big Bill. "What were you thinking, Bill?"

"Well, Hoople's obviously up to somethin' out there. I'm just afraid if he gets enough troops they might try and rush the building."

Sworski nodded gravely. "What do you suggest?"

"Well, there's only three ways into the building from down there: the two entrances out front, and the side door ... Those two doors are what worry me most, being mainly glass and all. But then they'd still have to come up the stairs into the foyer ... Suppose we try to stop 'em down there? Tell some a' the boys to go downstairs into the bar, grab as many beer bottles as they can handle, and then smash them all over those steps ..."

Jake was impressed at his father's quick thinking. Both he and Sworski knew the steps were made out of a hard, marble-like substance. Littered with jagged shards of broken glass, they would present a formidable obstacle. But Big Bill wasn't finished.

"And we'd still be on the higher ground … Get Tommy Rafftery and his boys stationed at the top of those stairs, and tell 'em to hose the steps down with the fire hoses …"

Sworski nodded thoughtfully. It was true there were high-pressure emergency hoses in two glass-fronted cases inset into the foyer walls—manned by hardy defenders who could hose down the slippery, glass-strewn steps, the building's most obvious weak spots might quickly become nearly impregnable. "And the side door?" he asked the elder McCool.

All three of them knew the door would admit only a single person at a time. It gave way to a long, steep flight of stairs, equally narrow, that rose to the back of the office floor, bypassing the first floor altogether.

"Simple," answered Jake's dad. "Get a bunch of the stacking chairs from the main hall, stand up here, and start throwin' 'em down at that door."

Sworski and Jake understood the ingenuity of this at once. Individually, each chair was a flimsy construction of tubular metal and cheap wood, barely strong enough to support the weight of a full grown man. But thrown willy-nilly down the steep stairway into a dense tangle against the crash-bar of the exterior side door, they would become a dense, immovable tangle.

"Get Tommy and his boys all set up, Spike, and they can take the early shift. Tell 'em my boy 'n me'll relieve 'em about midnight or so … We could be in for a long night."

Sworski nodded in agreement and rose to go back out onto the office floor to address his supporters, and to begin implementing Big Bill's stratagems. The girls were about to get the rest of the afternoon off. "Oh, and Spike? Wouldn't hurt to get somebody on the blower and get as many men in here as we can as quickly as possible. But tell 'em to get a move on— once we're barricaded in here nobody gets in—or out … Mind if I use your phone?"

Spike paused at the door to take in Bill McCool's parting words, and then he nodded. "No, of course not, Bill. Go right ahead."

Jake and his father were alone then, and Jake listened as his dad called his brothers—Jake's uncles— Bud and Walt. The conversations with each were basically the same: cursory descriptions of the crisis unfolding at the Hall, admonitions to act quickly, and to park well away from the Hall, on the side streets up in the West End in behind the Hall, and then to slip in through the back of the building, use the side entrance to come in. And plan to spend the night.

Outside meanwhile, Hoople's minions were loping swiftly down Elm Street. They paused impatiently at Lorne Street just long enough for the light to change and then resumed their urgent ramble toward downtown Sudbury. The pair separated at Durham Street, one man turning right, heading up Durham toward the Coulson, while the other continued down Elm, on his way to the Frontenac Hotel and the other dive bars that studded the old Borgia district like so many rotten teeth in an ailing jaw.

Hoople's orders to the pair had been simple enough: roust as many rubbies and rounders as possible and recruit them to swell the ranks of the dissident, though still small, throng he was assembling outside the Mine Mill Hall. Both his minions were dubious about their prospects; it would be difficult, after all, to lure a bunch of alkies away from a sure, steady supply of drinks in their familiar saloons out to the uncertain future of this impromptu event on the street outside the Union Hall blocks away up the Elm Street hill. Besides, Hoople's little hip flask was already running low. But Hoople had brushed these objections aside, with assurances that soon his troops would enjoy as much booze as they could handle— and free booze at that—once they had stormed the Hall and commandeered the basement bar. "Tell 'em that!" Hoople sputtered. "Tell 'em soon they'll have all the free drinks they could ever want if they'll just get their asses up here! Just get as many men up here as soon as you can! And while you're downtown use the pay phones to call as many of our guys as you can think of, tell 'em what's happening, and to get their asses back down here soon's they can! Got plenty a' dimes, you two? Well, get goin' then!"

It *was* a difficult chore—many of their would-be recruits had already spent a long afternoon in the downtown saloons, and greeted the entreaties of their would-be recruiters only with bleary eyes and stupefaction. But Hoople was proved right. The phrase "free booze" quickly captured universal attention, and soon it was on every man's lips, spreading from table to table like a sacred mantra. One by one the rubbies rose unsteadily to their feet and began straggling toward the exits.

Hoople was heartened to see that now his troops completely filled the sidewalk in front of the Hall and that the dense, milling throng would soon begin spilling out over the curb, and into the street itself. But so what if they caused a traffic jam? That was not his concern. So much the better if they snarled traffic. It would simply add to the chaos. Mischief was afoot, and, from Henry Hoople's standpoint, the more of it the merrier.

But as the hours passed by and it was growing dark, Hoople and his henchmen were becoming worried. The early, adrenal excitement of what they were doing was wearing off, and the crowd in front of the Mine Mill Hall was growing restive—and thirsty. Where was all this free booze they'd been promised? Maybe it was time to make their move? Hoople quietly summoned one of his chief lieutenants, Bill "Shakey" Akerley, a utility labourer in and around the Copper Cliff smelter complex. Akerley had earned his nickname as the result of the pronounced tremor in his hands, from one too many benders. Shakey probably no longer had a tooth left in his head and Hoople doubted if he could even read or write, which barely mattered in his job of sweeping the dusty smelter floors or shovelling up conveyor belt spills in the baghouse and sintering plant, and mattered not a damn to Henry Hoople right now, as he stood between his restless crowd and the inviting, mainly glass, front doors of the Mine Mill Hall.

"Listen, Bill," Hoople spoke softly into Akerley's ear. He couldn't help it, but the man invariably reminded him of the actor Walter Brennan, only Akerley was taller, and skinny. Akerley squinted at Hoople intently, "Yeah?" Hoople wished he'd never thought of the Brennan angle. "Bill, I want you to go up to the doors over there and look in. Then tell me what you see."

Akerley, hunched over as always, shuffled dutifully over to the doors.

Inside was Tommy Rafftery, who was poised and relaxed and had been waiting for just such a moment.

Rafftery had prepared by removing his upper, which concealed the loss of his front teeth in some now long-forgotten scrap. Tommy sat at the top of the front stairs, holding the nozzle of a fire hose over his shoulder like a bazooka that could be brought into play at a moment's notice. As soon as he sensed a movement outside the door he broke into a wide, malevolent toothless smile.

"Yeah, that's right, you potlickin' Pittsburgh piss-ant," he yelled. "Ya want some a' this? C'mon then, ya sleazy buncha gutless bastards, come right on in!"

Akerley couldn't hear Rafftery's words through the heavy plate glass of the doors, but the sight of it all—the toothless, leering smile below a pug's nose that had been broken countless times—the dark, glistening shards of broken glass on the slippery wet steps leading up to the fearsome Rafftery—was all Akerley needed to see. He hastily retreated back to the crowd.

"Rafftery 'n his goons is in there, Henry, all set up 'n waitin' for us to try 'n rush the place! They got the fire hoses out, and broken beer bottles all over them stairs!" he wheezed out excitedly, in a voice much louder than Hoople would have liked.

"Shhh! Lower your voice, Bill," Hoople tried to calm his hyperventilating confederate, who was now shaking in earnest. "We ain't going in that way!" Akerley declared, still loud enough to be overheard by the knot of protestors who, sensing something important was happening, had now huddled closely around to hear Akerley's report. "Leastways I sure ain't."

"There, there now, Bill," Hoople tried to soothe Akerley with a confidence he did not entirely feel inwardly.

"That Tommy Rafftery's crazier'n a shithouse rat, Henry, 'n I ain't goin' in there!" Akerley's voice rose to a high whine of protest.

"All right, all right Bill," Hoople replied, redoubling the tone of reassurance. Damn! But the damage was done, Hoople sensed, as news of Akerley's reconnaissance rippled through the crowd behind him. Clearly a frontal assault was out of the question. That left the side door.

Hoople turned to face the crowd, searching for a handful of faces he knew—and trusted. There weren't many. He certainly was thin on the ground if Shakey Akerley was one of his best men. But the newly arriving recruits from downtown were likely even less reliable.

Reluctantly Hoople pointed at Akerley once again. "All right, Bill, you and you and you and you" —he picked out faces almost at random—"you all come with me."

He led them, well away from the front door where he knew Tommy Rafftery awaited, around the corner of the hall and down the narrow passage that led to the side door. Soon, away from the street lights that illuminated the sidewalks in front of the Hall, they were enveloped in gloom, which gave the little expedition a spooky, surreptitious feel. Without being told, each man lowered his voice to a loud whisper. In about fifty yards they reached the side door. Hoople fully expected to find it locked, but to his surprise and delight he felt the solid wooden door give when he pushed on it. But then it jammed against something inside.

"It's not locked!" Hoople proclaimed in triumph. "But it's jammed on something just inside there ..."

"All right, you four men, push hard against it with your shoulders!" Hoople ordered in a stage whisper.

They did so, and once again the door gave way, momentarily sending hopes soaring among Hoople's little band. But after it was opened only a few inches, the door again encountered a rather spongy, mysterious resistance.

"Okay, now! Everybody push now! Aaaand hard! Harder! Aaand now! One more time, boys! Give 'er shit like nice!" But it was no use. The harder they pushed, the stouter the resistance became. Just as Big Bill had foreseen, the jumble of stacking chairs tangled against the door at the bottom of the staircase inside settled into a solid mass the more force was applied against them from outside.

Again and again the foursome strained against the door, to less and less effect. Hoople sighed. Clearly they would never gain access to the Hall this way. The front doors seemed equally difficult. But the Mine Millers were all trapped inside. Very well then. They'd just have to wait them out.

"Okay, okay boys, that's enough," Hoople whispered loudly, at last. "C'mon, let's go back around front."

Hoople and his little party headed back down the passageway toward Regent Street.

Back inside the Mine Mill Hall, meanwhile, events were unfolding much as Big Bill had recommended earlier. From the first floor below came the unmistakable sounds of beer bottles being hurled, with a dull popping sound and the occasional shattering of glass, against the hard steps leading up to the foyer from the street entrance, accompanied. eventually by the sweet, yeasty smell of beer wafting up from below.

But that was not the only smell rising from the bowels of the building. Soon there came a rich, savoury smell that quickly had noses twitching throughout the second floor offices where the Mine Mill loyalists had taken up makeshift residence.

"I asked Sammy to cook up a batch of his Irish stew," Spike explained. Everyone knew he was referring to old Sam Dwyer, the pensioner who ran the lunch counter in the basement of the Hall. The lunch counter served up cheeseburgers, hot dogs, fries and other short-order fare just outside the entrance to the tap room. Just the smell of Sammy's cooking lifted the spirits of the troops two floors above immensely, and before long word arrived that the stew was ready.

A general exodus began, and the occupiers were soon tromping down the stairs toward the smell of Sammy's hearty beef stew. As they did so, many of them glimpsed for the first time Tommy Rafftery and his boys sitting in the foyer, fire hoses at the ready. In one way it was a reassuring sight to see Rafftery and his toughs standing guard as their first line of defence. But in another way it was unnerving, too: there were few illusions about the near lethal beatings Rafftery and his pugs had administered in defence of the Mine Mill cause, and, as they trooped past on their way down to the floor below, it occurred to many of them, as it did to Jake himself, that if their besiegers ever did succeed in storming the Hall, very little quarter could be expected in the final, desperate clash. It was a sombre group that settled in over steaming bowls of Sam Dwyer's Irish stew. It now seemed highly likely that their impromptu action, which had begun with such joyous bravado, would end in bloodshed, even death.

30

The Siege
of the Mine Mill Hall

It was a revived and grimly determined group that returned back up to the office floor once their repast was finished. They settled in to await whatever might happen next. Their ranks had grown slightly; Jake's uncles were among the reinforcements who had slipped in through the side door just as dusk fell, and before the barricading had been completed. The police had also been called, though there were few illusions that Sudbury's finest would intervene on the side of the Mine Millers. They had, in fact, arrived at the scene, sirens blaring and cherry tops flashing, but instead of acting to clear Hoople's ever growing band, which was now spilling out onto Regent Street, they had simply set up shop at the corner of Regent and Elm, their cruisers drawn to a stop akimbo in the dead centre of one of the city's busiest intersections, where they established a roadblock, rerouting traffic around the congestion in front of the Mine Mill Hall on Regent Street.

Inside the Hall, someone had turned on one of the secretary's radios. As he idly tuned through the stations, a male voice became audible through the static. "This is Hartley Hubbs, CKSO Radio News, coming to you live from the front of the Mine Mill Union Hall ..."

"Hey, will ya get a load a' this!" interjected an occupier. "Listen up, everybody, we're on the news!"

The signal boomed in loud and clear—as it should have, the CKSO studios and transmitter tower were atop the Regent Street hill, mere blocks away—but the message was garbled, especially when Hubbs turned to Réjean Préfontaine, a randomly selected protester to explain, in his own words, why he was there. The place was full of Commies, there'd been an election, and they'd lost—no, not our side, the *Commie* side—and just why it was they were now inside the building while the winning side was left standing outside looking in he really wasn't sure, but ... His voice trailed off, and Hubbs thanked him briskly.

"Préfontaine!" an occupier spat out the name like a bad taste. "Anybody here know this knucklehead?"

Nobody did.

"Say, I bet he ain't even a member!" concluded an occupier who was stretched out uncomfortably on a sleeping bag on the hard floor. In this he was correct—Préfontaine had been lately recruited in the bowels of the Borgia only moments before, and Hoople, who had crowded up close to the radio reporter so he could hear every word, was impressed with Préfontaine's overall grasp of the subject, all things considered. The arrival of the radio man and the police cars up the street with their red lights throbbing ceaselessly—the strobing colour lent the scene a sense of lurid intensity—all of it ratcheted up the mood in his milling, expectant throng, much to Hoople's satisfaction.

The crowd, which had at first numbered only a few dozen, had now swollen to a few hundred, due mainly to Hoople's earlier recruiting efforts in the Borgia. But now, he sensed, the radio exposure was speeding things up, and he was delighted when Hubbs promised to return every hour, on the hour, to update his story.

Inside the Hall the occupiers continued to settle in for what promised to be a long and uncomfortable night. Their sense of isolation was now complete—the police could be expected to do no more than direct traffic, and now radios across the district were blaring out the news that their enemies had them trapped inside the Mine Mill Hall.

None of this was surprising, of course. The Sudbury cops, many of whom had begun their careers as company police officers, had never been friendly to organized labour. The same was true of the city's news media, so why expect anything different now? No, they were well and truly on their own, as they had been, in fact, since the Union was first organized. The hostility of the company was a given. Much of the locally owned small business community shared this antipathy, even though, in the view of Spike Sworski and many other union leaders, this position represented a misguided sense of self-interest. The Union's strength in bargaining, after all, had produced wage increases that resulted in ever-higher disposable incomes—money spent in the community and in the shops of the store owners who insisted on identifying their own interests with the company, rather than the Union, which bore them no ill will. As the early evening of the long night wore on, the occupiers of the Mine Mill Hall hunkered down, and an uneasy calm descended—it was still them against the world: so what else was new?

For his part, Big Bill McCool fought to stay awake, even as those encamped on the floor around him fell into noisome, restless slumber. McCool kept an anxious eye on his watch; the hours seemed to drag past.

Only Henry Hoople found time, that amazingly elastic, elusive quantum, passing more slowly. Outside on the sidewalk in the hours before midnight the dedicated anti-Mine Mill militant was beginning to wonder, for the first time, if he had bitten off more than he could chew. There was no mistaking the growing restiveness of his troops, who were becoming more sober—and less patient—by the minute. "Say Henry, where's all this free booze we was promised?" demanded Shakey Akerley, who was beginning to bear a more pronounced resemblance to his nickname with each passing moment, as the DTs set in. Christ! When was the last time he'd gone this long without a drink? Or at least, this long in the evening? It must've been Christmas Eve when, to the chagrin of Akerley and his fellow drinkers, the publicans of the Borgia had closed their establishments early, rousting their indignant patrons with a last call at two in the afternoon, leaving them to face the bleak rigours of withdrawal in the even bleaker surroundings of solitary skid row hotel rooms. And on Christmas Eve, when Christmas cheer with his own mates was what a man needed most! Was there no sense of Christian charity left in this world?

Hoople could only shrug helplessly in response to Akerley's query, which was, Hoople realized, as much plea as question. But what was he to do? The Hall's defenders had cagily barricaded themselves in, in such a way that Hoople and his rabble dared not tackle them head on. How much longer could he hold this mob together when, to a man, they longed so powerfully to drift back down the hill to their old familiar haunts, where they would once again be surrounded by their old bosom buddies of the bottle?

Inside the Hall Bill McCool decided at last it was time to wake his son. Carefully picking his way through the sleeping mass of his fellow occupiers, he approached Jake, stopping to tap him gently on the shoulder with the toe of his shoe. He didn't dare say anything, for fear he might wake the other sleepers. But his young lad only groaned softly, and remained sound asleep. Big Bill envied his youthful ability to sleep so deeply, despite such adverse circumstances. He tapped Jake's shoulder again, harder this time. "Jake!" he whispered. "C'mon son! It's our turn to stand watch!"

This time the younger McCool was stirred to wakefulness. Roused out of a warm and pleasant dream about Jo Ann Winters; even though they'd split up months ago, Jake still dreamt of her with fondness. But then, suddenly she was gone, and here he was on the floor of the Mine Mill Hall, being roused from sleep by his father. "Yeah, okay, okay, I'm coming, dad. Keep your shirt on!" Jake whispered as loudly as he dared.

He pulled himself out of his sleeping bag and, still half asleep, followed his father down the stairs to the first floor, where they found Rafftery and his confederates fighting off sleep themselves. A certain disturbance could be heard from outside the Hall, along with the crunching of footsteps on top of the canopy at one entrance.

"What's going on out there?" Big Bill asked Rafftery.

"Big crowd, gettin' bigger, and all worked up," Rafftery explained, relinquishing his chair and fire hose to Bill McCool. "But I doubt they've got the sand to make a rush straight at us. Still, ya never know, so look sharp down here, boys ... Thanks a lot for doin' this, brother."

Jake relieved the tired Mine Miller at the other door, while outside, to Henry Hoople's everlasting wonderment and gratitude, a sudden murmur rippled through the crowd; something was happening! It started with the flash of headlights on the edge of the crowd, in itself unusual, since the police had blocked off Regent Street hours ago. For some reason they had decided to let this vehicle through.

Hoople pushed his way through the crowd to the car. Its front passenger door opened and out stepped union president Bobby McAdoo. Hoople flushed with amazement and pleasure as he stepped forward to greet the newcomer, who was just finishing his cigar.

"Bobby! Am I ever glad to see *you!*" gushed Hoople, pumping McAdoo's hand.

"Henry," the union president replied evenly as he surveyed the scene. "Now what we got goin' on here, Henry?"

"Mine Mill son-of-a-bitches pulled a fast one on us, Bob. Went in and took over the Hall—but we got 'em surrounded!"

"I can see that. You're holding the old fort, eh, Henry? Good for you! But who *are* all these people?" McAdoo, a successful union politician with a remarkable memory for names and faces, had been scanning the crowd for familiar ones. With the singular exception of Shakey Akerley, he couldn't find anyone he knew.

Hoople shrugged, and lowered his voice. "Buncha guys from the Borgia. Rubbies mainly. Promised 'em booze to get 'em up here, but the fuckin' Commies have themselves so well barricaded inside we don't dare rush the place. Our troops are getting restless, Bob. Why don't you say somethin' to 'em, maybe tune 'em up, get their minds on other things?"

McAdoo, still sizing up the crowd over Hoople's head, chewed his stogie meditatively before responding.

"Yeah, sure thing, Henry. I can do that. Help me get up there?" McAdoo gestured at the flat canopy that covered the entrance to one of the Hall's front doors.

Hoople motioned at the driver to pull his car forward, nudging his way through the throng. When the hood was even with the front edge of the canopy, Hoople signalled a stop.

"Here ya go, Bob," Hoople offered a hand to McAdoo to help him clamber up on the vehicle's slippery front bumper. From there McAdoo scaled the hood and windshield before climbing on to the roof itself. Next it was an easy step on to the canopy. As Hoople knew, the newly elected union president was a riveting speaker, with a powerful voice that boomed out over the crowd and at once commanded its attention.

"Brothers and sisters!" yelled McAdoo, even though those milling about at his feet were, in fact, neither, in either the literal or figurative senses of the words.

"Brothers and sisters!" he repeated, motioning for calm, and, to Hoople's amazement, the entreaty appeared to work—the mob did seem to simmer down, almost despite itself. The effect was heightened as the car's driver backed up slowly before throwing on his high beams, illuminating McAdoo in the glare of the headlights.

It took McAdoo a moment to gauge his audience before he began to rake them over with that perverse genius common to demagogues everywhere: once he had the range, his aim for the tender spots left by a lifetime of neglect, privation and bitterness was unerring. Bob McAdoo knew well how to assay the darker planes of human existence.

"Brothers and sisters! Now I know you're wondering why it is that honest, God-fearing folks like yourselves are out here pounding the pavement, while a buncha' godless, atheistic Commie bastards is sleeping inside, under a comfortable roof tonight! And you know what?" Here McAdoo paused a beat for effect, as a murmur of approbation mixed with expectation rippled through the crowd.

"I wonder the same goddamn thing myself!" The mob roared its approval, urging McAdoo on. The union president began to pace the long, narrow canopy, working himself up as he dug deep, searching for just the right words to hurl at the crowd.

Hoople himself, happy to relinquish his leadership role, melted back through the crowd, which now filled both lanes of Regent Street, until he was on the very edge of the milling throng. He stood on the curb of the sidewalk adjacent to Queen's Athletic Field, where he was just able to see over the crowd massed before the Hall, which stood mesmerized by the pacing, fulminating McAdoo. To his right Hoople noticed that a police cruiser was silently gliding to a halt at the edge of the crowd, headlights and flashers off.

McAdoo stopped pacing at the lip of the canopy, ready at last to resume his peroration. He looked down into the thousand or more eager, expectant upturned faces. "So why *are* we out here? You're all good people, I know it, and I'm the legitimately elected president of the goddamned union!"

"There's just one answer: it's a Commie power grab, plain and simple! They don't believe in democracy, not here or in Communist Russia!"

At this point the police cruiser, which had arrived on the periphery of the crowd so inconspicuously, announced its presence by shining its powerful floodlight on McAdoo. The effect was of a follow-spot bathing a stage performer in a pool of light, greatly enhancing McAdoo's presence, adding gravitas to his speech. The crowd was now hanging on every word, and Henry Hoople thrilled at the drama of the moment.

"Hell no, they don't believe in free and fair elections! I won the last Local Union elections at 598 fair and square, and yet they're in there and I'm out here with you good people, all because an elite few think they know better than the majority of the membership! And isn't that always the way?"

Suddenly Hoople became aware of a flurry of activity at the base of the stainless steel flagpole which stood at the front of the Hall. Almost as suddenly the police spotlight panned away from McAdoo to a knot of protesters bunched around the flagpole. One of them was fumbling with the chain used to hoist the Canadian flag aloft, and in a moment Hoople could see why: a new flag was being raised up the pole, and thanks to the police spotlight, Hoople could see it for what it was—a red flag, adorned only with a yellow hammer-and-sickle! The flag of the Soviet Union was now flying over the Mine Mill Hall! It took a moment for the full significance of this to dawn on the assembled multitude, but they soon let out a whoop of derision as McAdoo gestured up at the red flag illuminated by the police spotlight.

"Isn't this always the way? An elite few always think they know what's best for everyone, and take what they want by force!"

"But is that how we want to live in Canada?" The crowd roared back with a single voice: "Noooo! Booooh!" "But here we are, in Sudbury, goddamned Canada, out in front of the only building in the entire Dominion that has the hammer-and-sickle flying over it, instead of our beloved Canadian Union Jack!" McAdoo paused for another beat, and the crowd responded with another roar: "Booooh!" McAdoo had found the range now, and he continued in a cadence calculated to fuel the crowd's simmering rage.

McAdoo's actions reinforced his words, punctuating the hectoring oratory he was using to prod and goad the crowd to action. At times he would even turn his back on them as he paced restlessly up and down the flat canopy that stretched from the front door of the Union Hall out nearly to the sidewalk that lined Regent Street. When that happened the crowd seemed to quieten, become a restless, yet respectful, shuffling mass, waiting as the great man searched to find his next words. And then, when he found them, he whirled to face the multitude, his dark eyes flashing as he strode catlike back toward the crowd.

From his vantage point across Regent Street Hoople surveyed the unfolding spectacle with wonder: how had this all happened? A few short hours ago he had paused, more or less on an instinctive hunch, to gather a half-dozen or so Steelworker supporters as they left the Hall in the late afternoon, and now this! He was thrilled at what had transpired—at the steadily growing mob of supporters who had swollen the ranks so spontaneously, at the sudden arrival of McAdoo, whose car was permitted to pass through a police cordon, at the appearance of Hubbs, whose hourly news updates were almost serving as paid commercials for the Steelworker cause, at the stealthy arrival of the police cruiser with its floodlight glaring, lighting up the hammer-and-sickle flag, enhancing the drama of the whole scene. Everything had happened as if on cue, organized by some unseen hand. It was, decided Henry Hoople, a devout Roman Catholic, divine intervention, and a further sign that their cause was just. He stuck his hands in the pockets of his trousers and stood tall and proud, enjoying this moment, the drama playing out before him, with an almost religious intensity.

McAdoo, meanwhile, spun on his heels, and advanced once again towards the crowd. "Oh, yes!" he roared, pounding a fist into the palm of his hand. "The godless Commies think they've got us beat! But what do *we* say about that?" "No!" "Shame!" "Bullshit!" the mob sputtered back.

McAdoo leaned forward, cupped a hand to his ear.

"Fuck them!" a single voice could be heard, screaming above the roar, and then came the startling, soul-satisfying sound of shattering plate glass as someone threw a heavy object through the front door of the Hall.

Hoople held his breath then, and kept his eye on the police car. A blood-curdling roar greeted the sudden sound of the glass breaking. The intensity level ratcheted up a notch. Any minute Hoople expected to see a policeman emerge from the cruiser, moving against the miscreant who had heaved the brick. But no such intervention was forthcoming.

Jake, who had been sitting with his chair tilted casually but comfortably back against the wall, now sat down with the chair squarely on the floor, instantly alert. He redoubled his grip on the fire hose. Adrenalin flowing and heart pounding, Jake was now wide awake.

He was still sitting that way when the second rock came crashing through the door his father was guarding. Big Bill was unmoved, which Jake found reassuring, but not surprising.

After that the sound of breaking glass became almost commonplace, as the mob, venting its frustration, began the systematic trashing of the Mine Mill Hall.

As the cool, fresh evening air began to draft into the building through all the broken windows, Jake reflected that it was a good thing the siege hadn't occurred a few months earlier—in winter the cold alone might well have forced them out of the building.

The noise of the mob—and even of McAdoo's hectoring voice—could now be clearly heard by both Jake and his dad. The mob had by now long since forgotten their thirst for booze.

Now, they were thirsty for blood.

31

The Siege Is Lifted

Outside the Hall there had been a subtle shift in the mood of the mob, Hoople sensed. As McAdoo continued to berate them and as the windows were systematically smashed out one by one, the rabble began to forget the compelling urge to return to their watering holes back down in the Borgia. No, this was something more important, bigger than any one of them, a transcendent moment that might happen only once in a man's lifetime. This was *history*, something more intoxicating even than booze. They were enlistees in some grand, sweeping—but real-life— drama, the likes of which Sudbury had never seen. McAdoo's histrionics had succeeded beyond Henry Hoople's fondest hopes, and Hoople himself joined in the shouts of approval and prolonged applause that greeted the union president as he finished his speech and hopped down on to the roof of the car that had brought him, retracing his steps back down on to the hood, the bumper, and, at last, back down on the ground, where he was quickly encircled by admiring, back-slapping well-wishers.

The crowd was now all for rushing the building, an impulse tempered by the assumption that Tommy Rafftery and his thugs still awaited, fire hoses at the ready, at the top of the entrance stairs. Jake and his father were, in fact, prepared to start blasting away with high-pressure jets of water at anyone foolhardy enough to come anywhere near the now windowless front doors. The force would have been sufficient to push any such would-be intruder back on his heels, but no one ventured close enough to test the McCools.

Instead, the mob turned its attention to a throwing contest, to see who could be the first to smash out the upstairs windows of the Union Hall. It wasn't easy. At first missiles would smash harmlessly to the right, and then to the left, of the target window. They would crash loudly, but to little effect, against the stout yellow brick façade of the fortress-like building on Regent Street. Each such attempt would be greeted by enthusiastic cheers or collective sighs of dismay from the crowd of onlookers. The first successful projectile was sent sailing through Spike Sworski's window by the most improbable of contestants, Shakey Akerley himself. His successful throw was greeted by a wild, joyous cheer that turned Shakey into an instant sidewalk celebrity, whose broad, toothless grin was captured for one rapturous moment in the glare of the police car floodlight as the crowd surged and swirled around him, slapping his back and hugging him warmly. It was, arguably, the highlight of Akerley's life.

"Hoople's alarm clocks," Jake muttered to his father as, one by one, the trashing of the building's windows continued to punctuate the silence around them. Big Bill simply grunted in response. The sound of breaking glass had now become so commonplace that Jake was no longer startled by the racket or the loud cheers that came after it. The wee small hours of the morning dragged slowly, as both sides settled in for an indefinite stand-off. Jake longed for daybreak as he fidgeted uncomfortably in his chair, trying in vain to ease the numbness in his backside. He didn't dare walk around, or even stand up for a moment, lest the bloodthirsty mob outside suddenly decide to rush the building. If he was this antsy, how much more difficult must this be for his old man? But the elder McCool sat stoically, his gaze fixed on the door in front of him, in a state of constant vigilance. Jake had to admire his father's single-minded determination to see this through. He might be way over his fighting weight and he smoked too much, but his father was still a tough old bird, Jake thought with admiration. The older man's stamina and determination helped maintain Jake's own resolve, which flagged often enough as he glanced at his watch, only to discover that few minutes had passed since the last time he checked. Jake's mind wandered aimlessly in the darkened boredom as the night dragged on. His thoughts strayed from one to another, scattershot.

"Dad, do you think we'll ever get back to fighting the company?" Jake asked finally, at last giving voice to his inmost thoughts and doubts.

"Eh? What's that, Son?" asked Big Bill, startled out of his own reveries.

"Well, you know, it's been four years now since we've negotiated a new contract—no raises, and the contract language hasn't changed ..."

"Oh." The same question had been front of mind and on the lips of many a Mine Mill veteran, and now here it was, out of the mouth of a babe. Big Bill swallowed. He found himself delivering the stock answer. "Well, son, if we can just get these friggin' Steelworkers off our backs and get the Local turned back right side up, a' course we'll get back to bargaining for a new agreement, you'll see ..."

The small hours were difficult for Henry Hoople, too. His crowd had quietened considerably since McAdoo had ended his harangue, and now, Hoople knew, the hour of truth was fast approaching: last call down below, in the Borgia.

The members of his mob knew it, too. Hoople could feel the growing tension as the downtown recruits wavered between hurrying back down the hill in time for one last drink, or staying put to see what would happen next.

A few began to drift away as the critical hour approached, and Hoople could overhear the casual conversations that preceded the defections.

"Hey Shakey! You comin' down?"

"Naw, reckon not. Think I'd rather stay here." Akerley flashed a toothless, and somewhat rueful, grin. Hoople marked the old rubbie's newfound fidelity to the cause, vowing to himself that it would not go unrewarded. Bill Akerley's finest hour.

Meanwhile, Jake digested his father's words. "Yeah, I guess so." He tried to sound positive, but even he could sense the undertone of doubt in his response.

Silence descended as both of the McCools returned to their respective nocturnal reveries.

Meanwhile in front of the Hall, Hoople's crowd continued to melt away. Not a serious concern—he still had enough troops to maintain the siege—but reinforcements were no longer arriving. Hoople's thoughts turned, suddenly, to Hartley Hubbs. The radio newsman was no longer maintaining the promised hourly vigil. But of course! CKSO had signed off for the night at midnight, so there'd be no further support coming from that quarter until morning. No big deal, Hoople rationalized. How many people would be listening to the radio at this hour, anyway? With no windows left intact in the building, even that form of sporting excitement had been exhausted.

Back inside the Hall the father-son dialogue continued. Jake contemplated his father's words in silence for a time, formulating a response. "Yeah, but won't McAdoo still be president when this is all over? I mean, come on, Dad, we can't stay here forever. We can't live here in the Mine Mill Hall!"

This time it was Big Bill's turn to mull a response. "No, but McAdoo did swear a solemn oath to uphold and protect the Mine Mill Constitution, an oath he's clearly violated now that he's been exposed as nothing more than a Steelworker front man. Even the courts agreed with that ..."

"Yeah, but Dad, he's still the democratically elected president! He's gonna sit in Spike's chair some day, no matter what."

"Maybe so, Son, but first let's just get through this night. Then we'll see what tomorrow brings ..."

"Okay, fair enough, Dad." Jake resumed his vigil in silence, as did his father. The brief dialogue had helped Jake pass the time, but not nearly enough. Would morning ever come? he wondered anxiously as he searched in vain for the first telltale lightening of the sky outside. Thank God they were this far advanced in the early spring, when the days were growing noticeably longer!

Nights were absolutely interminable in the depths of the Sudbury winter, when there was barely eight hours of daylight. This night was long enough, Jake thought, as he squirmed in his chair impatiently.

But what wouldn't Hoople's troops have given to trade places with Jake! They had been on their feet now since the evening, shuffling uncomfortably to change position, even pacing a bit here and there, but now, to a man, their backs ached constantly from the strain of standing for hours on the hard sidewalk outside the Hall. Hoople admired their fortitude. But then, a lot of them were war vets, combat troops who had endured considerable hardship in their time. At least the intervening years of swapping endless, rye-soaked war stories in the city's many Canadian Legion branches and Borgia dive bars hadn't entirely rounded those rough edges off, Hoople reflected gratefully.

"Hear that?"

Jake hadn't.

"Listen, Son." Big Bill cocked his head toward the outdoors.

Jake listened intently, and then heard, over the steady noise of the shuffling, coughing, muttering multitude what his father was referring to—the first timorous trills of birdsong!

"The dawn chorus, Jake. Just starting. Daylight won't be long now, you'll see."

Outside, it was Shakey Akerley who first noticed the change in the sky. He nudged the fellow next to him, "See that?" he nodded upward, toward the sky.

"Yeah! I do, by God! It's just starting to get light!"

Soon enough the distinctive flat light of daybreak was all around them. For the first time they were able to see the detritus of their all-night vigil—the sidewalk was littered with countless cigarette butts, discarded empty cigarette packs and sundry other garbage.

And the next thing Henry Hoople knew, there was Hartley Hubbs, microphone in hand once again, broadcasting live from the scene of the dramatic stand-off outside the Mine Mill Hall. The city, Hoople sensed, was beginning to wake up.

The tandem of daybreak and Hubbs combined to bring further novelty to the party—for the first time onlookers began to gather on the sidewalks and streets outside the Union Hall, swelling the crowd still further and creating even more congestion.

These newcomers, who were merely curious, idle early risers with no allegiance to either side in the dispute were soon joined by another party with a very distinct interest, Sheriff Gaston Lemieux. His unmarked and very nondescript grey Chevy pulled up beside the Sudbury police cruiser whose occupants had yet to emerge despite the night's riotous proceedings. Lemieux's was a largely symbolic position, a coveted patronage sinecure that included a comfortable courthouse office, a full complement of clerical and administrative staff to do his bidding and the certain knowledge that he would rarely have to emerge from the comfort and quietude of the courthouse to actually enforce the peace—there was a squad of bailiffs and deputies at his command to attend to that. Evictions and the processing of court orders were their usual bailiwick.

However, on this morning, Sheriff Lemieux, bespectacled in horn-rimmed glasses and wearing a bowler-like Stetson, did climb out of his car and take an immediate look around. For some reason his gaze soon came to rest on Henry Hoople.

"Who's in charge here?" he demanded evenly of Hoople, who merely shrugged and pointed in the direction of Bob McAdoo, who had just begun to puff contentedly on his freshly lit morning cigar.

Lemieux then approached McAdoo, repeating his question, only to have McAdoo, who struggled to suppress his irritation at this interruption of his peaceful morning smoke, point grudgingly back at Hoople. "I dunno, Sheriff Lemieux, I swear I don't. Never seen most of these people before in my life. They were all out here when we got here. Hoople over there—Henry Hoople—he's your man." McAdoo appeared the very soul of wounded innocence.

Lemieux was an easy-going type, but he was becoming visibly irritated by the runaround as he returned to Hoople. "Now listen here, Hooper—"

"Hoople," interjected Hoople.

"Okay, Hoople," corrected Lemieux. "I want to know what's going on here. These people just can't be out here blocking the street like this."

Hoople looked the lawman up and down. Even with the Stetson, Lemieux barely came up to Hoople's chest. Hoople nodded agreeably, decided to play for time.

"Yessir, there Sheriff, I see your point all right. But the thing is, these people just showed up here last night, of their own accord, to engage in a free and democratic protest against the godless Communism that is threatening our free and democratic, God-fearing society."

Lemieux frowned and nodded impatiently. "That may be, son, but you've made your point. I want these people cleared off the street in five minutes, or so help me I'll read the Riot Act, swear to God I will!"

The confrontation between the sheriff and Hoople drew the interest of Hartley Hubbs, who, microphone in hand, was making his way through the crowd, pausing at intervals to interview random bystanders, drawing ever closer to Hoople and the bespectacled sheriff. Hubbs could sense that the real news was being made by whatever was transpiring between the lawman and the union man. But the tense dialogue was already drawing to a close by the time Hubbs reached the pair. "Five minutes, got that?" Hoople nodded reassuringly, and Lemieux spun on his heels and returned to his idling Chevy. "Troubles, Henry?" Hubbs inquired mildly of Hoople, shoving his mic in Hoople's face.

"Naw, Hartley, nothing we can't handle ... Now listen here, you folks, we need you to step back a bit, over across the street ..." Hoople turned to the crowd with his arms outstretched, attempting to herd them away from the front of the building. But he had earlier sown the seeds of discord, and now he was reaping the whirlwind. In the cold light of morning his troops were tired, disgruntled and thirsty—in no mood to follow orders, and even as one section of the crowd yielded dutifully before his outstretched arms, another, sullen and just as large, would surge in to take its place. It was, Hoople quickly realized, like herding cats, and he soon gave up the attempt.

Lemieux watched Hoople through the windshield of his patrol car with growing impatience. He climbed out of his vehicle a few minutes later and approached Hoople once again, this time clutching a sheaf of papers. At the same time Lemieux's deputy walked to the back of the squad car and opened the trunk. He reached in and pulled out some kind of weapon—it looked like a shotgun with an oversized barrel to Hoople—and broke it open, inserting a cylindrical canister into the breach. The gesture was not lost on Hoople—the sheriff was prepared to loose tear gas on the unruly, milling crowd.

"Now see here, Hoople. We've got rush hour about to start out there," Lemieux gestured at the city that lay around them in the greying dawn, "and we've got to have this street re-opened! I gave you time, and fair warning, to move these folks along, but nothing much happened, so now I'm going to read the Riot Act."

Lemieux began to read aloud from the papers in his hand, raising his voice in a vain attempt to make himself heard above the growling murmur of the tired, testy crowd.

"Our Sovereign Her Royal Highness Queen Elizabeth the Second chargeth and commandeth all persons, being assembled, immediately to disperse themselves, and peaceably depart to their habitations, or to their lawful business, on the pains contained in the Act made in the first year of King George the First for preventing tumult and riotous assemblies.

"GOD SAVE THE QUEEN!" Lemieux concluded at the top of his lungs.

A few of the rabble within immediate earshot began to respond to the royal salute by rote, repeating the words in a raggedly cadenced chorus before the full meaning of the ancient message began to sink in. They had no habitations, to speak of, to depart to, and certainly no lawful business. "God save the—aw, fuck you!"

"Yeh, God bugger the Queen!"

"Better yet, why don't *you* go bugger the Queen?"

General mirth bubbled up around these rejoinders, and Hoople foresaw nothing but trouble. He moved quickly over to McAdoo. "They're gonna teargas us, Bob! We gotta move these people outta here right now!"

McAdoo yanked the half-smoked stogie from his mouth, threw it down in disgust, and ground it into the pavement with the sole of his shoe. Another perfectly good morning smoke wasted.

"All right, all right, Henry." he growled. "I'll take as many of 'em as I can fit in my car."

Both men began to herd the demonstrators into McAdoo's car, which led the shuffling, disgruntled procession up Regent to Elm Street, and back down the hill towards downtown.

Inside the Mine Mill Hall, morning found the occupiers emerging from the warm but uncomfortable cocoons of their sleeping bags, stretching tiredly after a night's sleep that had brought all the peaceful repose of an all-night bombing raid.

Foley Gilpin, who had elected to spend the night inside the Hall, was happy just to be alive. He walked stiffly to the door of Sworski's office, knocked and entered.

Spike was already awake, listening to Hartley Hubbs' news bulletins on CKSO.

"'Morning, Foley ... Well, if this is all the work of the CIA as you claim, they didn't need to start up their own radio station. Voice of Freedom, was it?

"Liberation," interjected the newspaperman.

"Yes, well, whatever. They've no need, anyway, because they've got CKSO! They haven't stopped pumping up this nonsense," Sworski gestured toward the jagged outline of what had been his office window, "since it all started last night."

"True enough," Gilpin reflected. "But remember, Spike, ever since the raids started Steel has been one of the station's biggest advertisers, what with all the air time they've bought to take out ads smearing Local 598, and you personally. As one of my wisest colleagues said recently 'Freedom of the press belongs to those who own one.'"

"Yeah?" replied Sworski, rubbing his bloodshot eyes with both hands, "He sure knew what he was talking about. We gave it our best shot, old friend, but it just always seemed like no matter what we did, we always came up a day late and a buck short against 'em."

Gilpin did not disagree, but instead he cautiously approached Spike's busted-out window.

"Pretty well deserted out there now, Spike. Guess they've had their fun and gone home." Traffic was even beginning to stream slowly past on Regent Street, Gilpin noticed. Very slowly, given that it was the boomtown's usually manic rush hour; rubberneckers, Gilpin guessed, curious to inspect the Union Hall after the well-publicized events of the night before. The place must have looked like a bombed-out building. The hammer-and-sickle still fluttered, mockingly, in the morning breeze.

To this day, Foley Gilpin cannot quite explain what it was that first tweaked his attention ... just a vague *something* over on the other side of Queen's Athletic Field, so far away in the uncertain early morning light he could barely make it out ...

Gilpin glanced back around Sworski's office, and he spotted Spike's high-powered field glasses. "Mind if I use these?"

Sworski merely shrugged. "Knock yourself out."

Gilpin quickly grabbed the binoculars and returned to the gaping, jagged window. He removed his eyeglasses and laid them on the corner of Spike's desk before pointing the binoculars at the indistinct objects that had first drawn his attention, twisting the gnarled focus knob to gain a sharp focal plane. They were a powerful instrument, and Gilpin found it difficult to hold the binoculars steady enough to see clearly. Just breathing seemed to throw him off, as often as not. But then suddenly, as if by magic, the newspaperman succeeded in coordinating the necessary conditions all at once, at least for a split second. And then he saw with sudden, foreshortened crystal clarity: two figures standing side by side, the shorter one in a rumpled, nondescript trench coat, the taller one angular, athletic, in blue jeans and a grey, hooded sweatshirt. It was him! The mystery man—he was almost certain! It took Gilpin's breath away, and the field glasses jiggled ever so slightly and the frame was lost.

Exasperated, Gilpin pulled the binoculars away from his eyes, snatched his spectacles from Sworski's desk, and put them on before squinting at the distant figures in the hope he could get a better aim for another look. He snatched his specs off his face once again, peered through the binocular eyepiece, twisting the focus knob this way and that. But it was no use. Either the view was in focus and the frame was lost, or everything was so blurry that there was no frame, to speak of, at all. Finally, Gilpin gave up at his attempt for a close-up view, and put his eyeglasses back on. Once again, he peered across the athletic field. Yes, they were still there, no doubt about it. This was *not* a figment of his imagination.

Across the distance of Queen's Athletic Field a pair of solitary figures stood watching the front of the

Mine Mill Hall. Clearly, the night-long siege was drawing to a close. The shorter observer, the one wearing a trench coat, was scanning the front of the Union Hall with his own binoculars. *"There,"* he pronounced with satisfaction. "That'll give 'em something to remember, 'stead of your little, ah, misadventure in that alley downtown last summer. What *were* you thinking?"

His companion shrugged. "I didn't like the little shit-face. Those snot-nosed college kids are gonna be big trouble, and I don't mean just for the Agency. They're gonna jeopardize the entire war effort before they're done, maybe even the President ..."

Trench Coat looked up at him in disbelief. "So we go around kicking the crap outta them? *That's* your solution?"

"Spoiled brats," averred the athletic figure, who stood with his legs stretched wide and his arms crossed over his chest. "We don't dare slap 'em around down there." A note of contempt entered his voice. "All the bleeding hearts would be raising bloody hell if we did. Look, we're gonna have to deal with punks like that eventually, I just thought this place and that time would be more convenient ..."

Trench coat emitted an audible groan. "You *thought?* *You* thought? For Chrissakes, this isn't Berlin in '45! Please do me the favour of *not* thinking when you're in the field. Simply following orders would suffice. Got that?"

The tall figure simply shrugged. "Sure. Whatever you say. Now get me outta this shithole. What time's our flight?"

"Wheels up fifteen minutes after we're on board." They turned away and descended the embankment above Alder Street, heading for Elm Street and, eventually, their next assignment in defence of the free world.

Big Bill McCool and his son Jake adjourned to Gus's Restaurant just up the hill and around the corner from the Union Hall on Elm Street for breakfast once it was clear that the siege had lifted and the threat to the Union Hall and its occupants had wound down.

Both men were bone-tired, the adrenalin of the night's events now having long since worn off. They settled in to a booth at Gus's surrounded by the restaurant's familiar morning smells of freshly brewed coffee and frying home fries.

Soon, both of them were holding mugs of steaming hot coffee.

Jake raised his first. "Well, Dad, here's to the Mine Mill."

Bill McCool tapped his mug against his son's.

The younger man looked into his father's eyes. "But I think we're beat, Dad."

Father returned his son's look with a steady, world-weary gaze.

"I know it, Son."

"But at least we lived to tell the tale, as Uncle Bud would say."

"And to drink more of Gus's bad coffee."

Both men laughed out loud. It *was* good to be alive, and breathing the old familiar aroma of home fries and onions being cooked back in the kitchen here at Gus's.

"There were times last night I wasn't sure we'd make it," Jake confessed to his father.

Big Bill nodded sheepishly. "I know. I'm very sorry I got you into that, Son. But when I called the mine yesterday I had no way of knowing ..."

Jake cut his father off with an upraised hand. "I know, Dad. I know." It seemed an age ago that Jake had received the summons from his dad to join him at the Mine Mill taproom, but in fact it was only yesterday. So much had changed in so little time! Jake surveyed the world outside Gus's windows with bleary eyes—everything appeared slightly fuzzy and out of focus, somehow.

Jake's father shook his head. "And if your mother ever got wind of this I'd never see the inside of the old homestead again."

The statement was, Jake realized, only a slight exaggeration. His mother had warned him off involvement in the Steel raids from the start. But now that they had both survived last night's harrowing experience, Jake felt it was a new day, in more ways than one ...

"Listen, Dad, there's something I've been meaning to talk to you about ..."

Big Bill nodded agreeably. "Go ahead, Son."

"Dad, I think it's time I moved out, got a place of my own."

The elder McCool frowned. "But where would you live? Housing's mighty tight around town right now, Jake."

"I know. But Foley Gilpin says he has a spare bedroom, and that I'm welcome to bunk in with him until I find a place."

Big Bill considered this with pursed lips before nodding his head slowly. "Very well, Son. You're a grown man now, been doing a man's job for what, almost a year now. I certainly won't stand in your way if that's what you really want ... What say we order some breakfast?"

They emerged from the restaurant into uncertain Sudbury spring sunshine an hour later.

"I'm going back to the Hall before I head home," Bill explained to his son. "To say goodbye to Bud and Walt."

Jake accompanied his father for the short walk to the Mine Mill Hall, but he felt reluctant to re-enter the building with his dad. It just seemed to Jake all of a sudden like a place with too much history and too little future.

"Well Dad, guess I'll leave you here. I think I'll walk over to Foley's—let him know I've decided to take him up on his offer. Tell Mom what we talked about. I'll be out to the Valley later to start moving my stuff."

Big Bill turned, surprised. "What? You're not coming in? All right, Son. I'll explain things to your mother."

The two men faced each other, shook hands, and after an awkward pause, embraced each other as people will do when they are on the cusp of great change and facing an uncertain future.

Bill McCool patted his son lightly a few times on the back before holding him out at arm's length to get a good look at his boy. He liked what he saw.

"Take care of yourself, Son."

"I will, Dad. I promise."

Jake found Gilpin's building—an aging, unprepossessing red brick place on a side street just a short walk from downtown—and he climbed a few flights of stairs to reach his friend's apartment. The hallways of the building had a steamy ambience and were redolent of bacon frying and coffee brewing. Jake tapped softly on Foley's door, and his friend answered almost at once.

"Jake!" The newspaperman was not displeased at the interruption—he still had few friends in the city, and visitors were always welcome. "Come in, come in!"

"I was just making some fresh coffee. Come on in and sit down in the kitchen. Care for a coffee?"

"No, no thanks. I've just come from Gus's with my dad, so I'm pretty much coffee'ed right out."

Within minutes of seating himself at Gilpin's kitchen table Jake came right to the point. "Listen, Foley, remember how you once told me if I ever wanted to leave my folks and move into town I could crash here until I found my own place?

"Well, after last night I think that time has come ... Mom's gonna figure out Dad and me were in on that pretty fast, and life won't be worth living out there for either one of us ..." Jake grinned awkwardly.

Gilpin smiled sympathetically. "So get out while the getting's good, eh, Jake? Sure, I get it, and my offer still stands ... We'll split the rent fifty-fifty—your end'll be twenty five bucks a month, plus utilities—

and you can have the spare bedroom ... I'll move my office outta there into the living room and it'll be all yours ... Come 'ere and I'll show you around ..."

The truth was Foley Gilpin was delighted by this news. His freelance income was still minimal and the chance to save on rent and household expenses was a godsend. Besides, he'd like the company—he'd always enjoyed Jake's easygoing ways and youthful swagger, and his knowledge of a city where Foley himself was still learning the ropes.

The apartment tour didn't take long—the place consisted of the kitchen, living room, bathroom and two bedrooms—and what Jake noticed was that the apartment, with dull, hardwood floors and equally dull, beefy old-school baseboards, and porcelain bathroom fixtures that were no longer gleaming, appeared homey, well lived in and not overly tidy— Gilpin seemed to have newspapers, books and note-books strewn over every flat surface of every room. A quintessential bachelor pad. But the *pièce de résistance* was a six-foot high stack of dusty newspapers, leaning precariously to one side, beside the fridge. "Just keepin' them there 'til I get around to clipping 'em for my files," Gilpin explained.

None of this mattered a great deal to Jake, for whom the flat held the twin attractions of freedom and hominess. "You got yourself a deal—and a new roommate," he told Gilpin, offering his hand across the kitchen table.

They shook on it, and so began a new—and quite eventful—chapter in the life of Jacob Hamish McCool.

32

A Night on The Town

Summer burst brilliantly over the Basin that year, as it sometimes does, like a bomb. The city was transformed almost overnight, it seemed, from a frigid, barely habitable place of seemingly endless winter to a steamy, benign, infinitely forgiving climate. The ice was gone from the lakes and the sap was rising.

The new roommates settled easily enough into their new routine, alternating shopping and cooking duties on the rare evenings they didn't elect to eat out downtown somewhere—the China House and the Trevi Tavern were two especially favoured venues—when no one felt like cooking.

But it was one evening after they'd eaten at home that Foley touched on a subject he'd been wanting to broach with Jake for some time.

"So whatever happened between you and your girlfriend, Jake?" Gilpin sensed at once he'd struck a tender nerve.

Jake pulled a long face and shook his head. "I dunno, Foley, it just didn't work out, is all ... You know the reason better than anyone …" His voice trailed off, and Jake looked down, brushing crumbs off the kitchen table.

"You mean that caper at the President last summer?"

Jake swallowed, and nodded. The corners of his mouth drooped downwards. It was impossible for him to conceal that he still harboured feelings for Jo Ann Winters. He still missed her terribly.

Jake's lack of eye contact did not escape Foley, who looked closely at his young friend.

"Jeez, Jake, maybe you're being too hard on her—and yourself. Whatever was going on there—and we never did get to the bottom of that—whatever it was, it sure wasn't her fault …"

"Listen, ever since you moved in I've been watching you mope around—you go to work, come home, watch some TV and go to bed. That's it! That's all you ever do, day after day! You need to get out more, young fella your age, you should be going out at night, have some fun! All work and no play—"

"Makes Jake a dull boy." Jake finished, smiling despite himself. He was surprised, and more than a little touched, at his friend's evident concern for him. "Yeah, yeah, I get it Foley. I get it, I do. But after what happened to my brother I just didn't feel I could go back to her … There were just so many things between us we couldn't really talk about after that …"

"I know, kid, I know, but I hate to see you still beating yourself up over that … Maybe you should at least give her one more chance …"

Jake nodded uncertainly. He was a little surprised to discover he felt a lump in his throat. He smiled half-heartedly at Foley. "Yeah, maybe so, Foley. I guess you're right." And with that he stood up from the table, excused himself and went back to his room.

Jake unzipped the bottom of the case and pulled Ben's guitar out. He'd bought a songbook or two that contained, in the simplest possible terms, the music to a few of his favourite Dylan songs. After mastering a few basic chords—G, D and E—Jake had learned to strum out an accompaniment to his own homespun warbling of a few lyrics. On this night he sang "Honey, Just Allow Me One More Chance" before switching over to "Girl From the North Country."
Last year's *Freewheelin'* album by Bob Dylan always reminded him of Jo Ann. It was still one of his favourites. He put the guitar away and pulled the album from its well-worn slip cover before placing it on the turntable. With a heavy sigh Jake sat back on the bed to absorb Dylan's scratchy vocals for the umpteenth time ...

After a few more such morose, sorrowing weekday evenings Jake could stand it no more, and he ventured out on the town on Friday night.
Downtown Sudbury was a lively place on warm summer weekend evenings as young men, flush with their bonus earnings, stalked the Durham Street sidewalks toward their favourite haberdashers in search of new clothes. Often they'd enter the chosen menswear store clad in their old clothes and emerge a few

minutes later attired head to toe in brand new duds after instructing the clothier to simply burn the old ones. The scene on Durham Street itself was just as extravagant as youthful miners cruised back and forth from the Elgin Street strip to Christ the King in an endless river of polished chrome and revving V-8s fuelled by surging testosterone and thirty-cent-a-gallon gasoline.

Jake himself was drawn to gentler and cheaper—if not always much quieter—pursuits, to the live music venues that were beginning to proliferate in a downtown entertainment district geared increasingly toward a youthful population with both time and money on its hands, and on this night he chose to sample a new local rock 'n' roll band playing in the Bavarian Room of the old Nickel Range Hotel on Elm Street. The music itself was derivative—nothing Jake hadn't heard on the radio a million times before—Beatles tunes, mainly, interspersed with chanted incantations like "Louie Louie Lou-eye Hey, Hey! Hey, Hey! We Gotta Go!" but it got the packed house roaring along. The joint was jumping, and the air was overheated by the exertions of hundreds of over-amped, sweaty young people bobbing up and down, yelling out the hokey refrain at the top of its collective lungs. Jake himself, beer in hand, was feeling no pain when he sensed a soft tap on his shoulder. He turned around to see who it was, and almost died.

"Heya, Sparky. Goin' anywhere later?"

At first he couldn't believe his eyes and ears, but there was no doubt he was staring into the familiar green eyes of Jo Ann Winters. Of course she looked different now—her chestnut-coloured hair was longer and half-hidden beneath a peasant-style head-scarf, except for the few strands that had escaped and fallen around her shoulders. Her eyes were half hidden, especially in the dim light of the nightclub, behind a pair of rose-coloured, rectangular granny glasses, and she was clad in denim from head to toe in a funky workshirt and a long skirt that nearly touched the floor—but it was unmistakeably her, and Jake reached out for her instinctively, partly because she looked so good and partly to steady himself because he felt his knees buckling in the welter of emotion, the heat of the crowd and the steady throbbing of the kick drum and bass guitar.

She caught him, and pulled him close.

"Whoa, Jake! Are you all right?"

"Yeah, yeah, I'm fine ... Just surprised, is all ..." He held her out at arm's length for a better look. "You look great! Different, but great ..."

"You don't look so bad yourself there, sailor," and there was the same teasing laugh and mischief behind the eyes that still made him feel weak in the knees. It always reminded Jake of a line he'd picked up from a Russian poet in some half-forgotten but wholly disliked high school lit class: *Women who laugh and remind us that we are men ...*

They stayed that way, swaying together to the music, clinging to one another, until after last call and the house lights went up, forcing them abruptly out of their trance-like state.

They retreated together to Jake's place, which they had all to themselves because Foley was out for the evening. Jo Ann made a beeline for the living room stereo Jake shared with Foley, sorting through their LP collection, which was housed in a plastic milk crate. She quickly selected one, and turned to show it to Jake. He saw she was holding up *Freewheelin'*.

"Remember when you first heard this one?"

"Oh yeah, of course." Jake settled into an armchair. How could he ever forget? Hard to believe it had only been just over a year ago—so much had happened since! Some of it good, some of it not so much …

Jake forced himself to shake off the memories to focus on the here and now and the fact that Jo Ann was *here*, in his living room, as tall and willowy as ever.

She crossed the room to sit astride the wooden arms of his chair, hitching up her long skirt, facing him—her legs were long enough that she could sit comfortably in Jake's lap with her feet touching the floor, effectively pinning him into the chair. She reached into the breast pocket of her denim work-shirt and extracted what looked like a skinny, hand-rolled cigarette.

"Ever smoked dope, Jake?" And there was that mischievous grin.

"Uh, no, but it looks like I'm about to …"

"Wanna try it?"

"Sure, why not?"

Jo Ann inserted the skinny cigarette into her mouth, wetting it between her lips in the most unmistakably suggestive gesture Jake had ever seen in such close quarters. He was instantly aroused.

She pulled the moistened joint from her lips and placed the tip of it in her mouth before lighting it; an acrid, skunky smell filled the close space between them, and for Jake the universe had suddenly shrunk to the dimension of this one time and space, this one chair. At the same time he felt self-conscious because of his erection, and overcome by shyness. He hoped she wouldn't feel it.

Jo Ann sucked deeply on the burning joint before grasping it between her thumb and forefinger and passing it over to Jake. At the same time she had begun to rock back and forth over Jake's crotch. She was feeling it, all right.

Jake inhaled on the joint and quickly began to choke on the unfamiliar, acrid taste of the stuff. He did his best to hold it in, but he soon began to sputter and cough, the hot smoke billowing right back out through his mouth and nose.

Jo Ann had a hearty laugh at his expense. "Oh no, Jake! You just blew your toke! What a waste!"

Once again she took a deep drag off the joint, closing her eyelids against the acrid smoke, before passing it back to him.

This time he was more cautious, taking care to temper the smoke by inhaling cool air around it, and this time he succeeded in pulling the marijuana smoke—or most of it—deep into his lungs. He held his breath as best he could before exhaling slowly. He waited for some special sensation but, disappointingly, he felt none.

"I don't feel anything, Jo. Maybe this stuff isn't that good ..."

"Shh, Jake, don't be silly." She touched his lips with a cautionary upraised forefinger. "This is the very best dope to be found anywhere on campus ..."

"Campus! Where—What campus? Where *have* you been, Jo?"

She answered with a shrug. "Ryerson, in Toronto. After Daddy died, Mom never really got over it. She passed away just a few months later ... They left me some money for tuition, so after I graduated high school I enrolled at Rye High."

"What did you study down there?"

"Nightlife on Yonge Street mainly, but I chose Photography as a major."

"Sorry 'bout your mom." He hadn't heard a thing. Normally it was his mother who read the obits and kept him informed, but they'd all been so caught up in the raids ...

"Thanks. With both my folks gone and being dumped by my boyfriend, there wasn't really anything keeping me in Sudbury, so I decided to split ..."

"What? Oh, yeah ..." Although she was sitting on top of him it suddenly felt as if Jo Ann was talking over some grand distance, and in a language that he didn't immediately understand. He couldn't take his eyes or mind off the buttons on Jo Ann's shirtfront, now mere inches away from his face. The top two were unbuttoned, exposing her throat and, tantalizingly, the top of her chest. What, he wondered, would happen if he reached up to unbutton more of them? It was something that part of him longed—even ached—to do, but also something another part of him deemed an impossibly bold gesture.

Finally her words sank in—the part about the boyfriend. Jake felt he must say something. He reddened in confusion, his inward desires at odds with the discomfort of being called out so, and of having caused her so much pain …

"Oh, yeah, about that … I didn't mean to dump you Jo, really I didn't, but it was just that when that thing with Ben happened I …" his voice trailed off. He had gone as far as he dared.

"Shhh, Jake, it's okay, baby …" Jo Ann assumed he was talking about their bizarre parking episode, that night at the slag pouring. She plucked the reefer from her mouth and put it right back in between her lips lit end in first, somewhat to Jake's alarm. Then she brought her face close to his, leaning forward while gently cradling his head in her hands. "It's okay, Jake, let's get you stoned … Here, open your mouth …"

He did as instructed, more confused now than ever, and she blew a stream of red-hot marijuana smoke directly into his mouth. It burned the back of his throat, but Jake gulped back as much of it as he could.

"That's called shotgunning," she informed him after she quickly removed the joint from her mouth.

Jake could only nod his head in wordless wonder. His head was spinning at all that was happening, at the nearness of her, at the thought of those tantalizing buttons.

"You—you've changed, Jo."

She laughed lightly. "So have you! But yeah, it was good to get away, see different things. There's a lot happening out there, Jake ..."

Jo Ann was continuing to rock back and forth over his crotch in time with the Dylan songs on the album, and Jake felt a kind of pink, happy glow wash over himself. At last he reached up for her buttons, which he unfastened one by one. She did nothing to stop him, only looking down to watch and, if anything, grinding herself across his lap even more ardently.

He stopped after four or five buttons, and the shirt-front parted of its own accord, revealing Jo Ann's breasts. They weren't very large, but the sight still took his breath away, and he reached up to cup them gently in his hands. His work-roughened hands against the warm, rounded smoothness of her gave her goosebumps and he could feel her shiver as she pressed down on him even harder, riding him now ever faster. He gently tweaked her nipples between his thumb and forefingers and she grinned almost half-apologetically at him. "Still not much there, eh Jake? But you know what they always say—More than a handful's a waste!"

He pulled her to him then and stood up. She wrapped her legs around him and somehow he managed to get them into the bedroom, unsteady as he was with the room starting to spin and the sudden onrushing unsteadiness of the dope washing over him. He stumbled into the next room and they fell awkwardly together onto the softness of the bed, which struck Jake as hilariously funny somehow ...

Jo Ann was laughing, too, as they landed, but she still managed to land on top of Jake, and he just laid back and watched and felt what he felt as she opened his shirt and pants and climbed up on him before guiding him gently but surely inside her.

"You—you've done this before!" It was both a sudden epiphany and a statement.

She had removed the granny glasses and she looked him straight in the eyes, with a sober, thoughtful expression as she moved against him. "Maybe," she smiled shyly. And that was all the talking they did, communicating instead by caress and steady, tender wide-eyed gaze, and by touch as his sandpaper-rough hands scraped against the smooth, lean curving roundness of her, arousing shivers and shakes wherever they touched and wherever they wanted in their wandering wanton way. Sandpaper over satin ... She was so wonderfully responsive to him, so lean and tall and lithe that her nerve ends must be very near the surface, Jake realized, in what was his last coherent thought before he was thrusting up into her there! and there! and, oh Lord there! and he was utterly spent, spasmed out and breathless with exertion and wordless wonder.

"Oh Jo Ann, I've missed you so," he told her finally after he'd caught his breath.

"I never forgot you, either, Jake," she confided, looking deep into his eyes.

Foley positively beamed at them the next morning when he found them both at the kitchen table, still bathed in the morning-after afterglow that was a telltale sign to Gilpin.

"Hey, Jake! Good night?" he grinned at his youthful roommate.

"Not bad," Jake deadpanned, barely suppressing the urge to wink, before catching himself. "Uh, Foley, this is Jo Ann Winters. Jo Ann, this is my roommate, Foley Gilpin." Such formal introductions were rare among Sudbury's working-class men, who usually regarded them as both pretentious and unnecessary. That it was volunteered now by Jake was both an earnest sign of the affection he felt for both Foley and Jo Ann and a good omen.

Gilpin poured himself a coffee and pulled up a chair to join Jake and Jo Ann at the table.

Jo Ann smiled shyly at Gilpin. "So", she began, "Jake tells me you're a reporter ... Who do you work for?"

"*The Globe and Mail* in Toronto, mainly. I do a bit of freelance work for them."

"Foley's a real veteran," Jake interjected. "Big-time American papers, investigator, and everything."

"Really!" Jo Ann seemed impressed, and then became pensive. "How odd ..."

"Why odd?" queried Gilpin.

"Because I had a visit from an investigator just yesterday ..."

"About what, if you don't mind me asking?"

"He was an insurance investigator, interested in the way my daddy died ..."

"Oh?" Gilpin looked over at Jake, who now took a sudden interest in the conversation.

"But that was almost a year ago now, Jo. I would've thought all that would've been settled long ago ..."

"Oh, it was ... The insurance company paid out on Daddy's policy just a few months after it happened ... Of course, Mommy passed not long after that, so most of the money came to me ..."

"So I don't get it," Gilpin frowned. "What's left to investigate?"

Jo Ann shrugged. "Well, all I know is this investigator told me that new information has come to light ..."

"What sort of new information?" Gilpin pressed.

"Oh, some kind of new eyewitness to what happened," replied Jo Ann. "Apparently he claims it wasn't an accident, after all."

"Not an accident!" Jake exclaimed. "But what else could it have been?"

Jo Ann shrugged once again, wide-eyed in disbelief. "Now they're saying that maybe Daddy was pushed in front of that bus ..."

"But who'd want to do such a thing?" Jake wondered. "Your dad was such a mild-mannered guy ..."

"I know," agreed Jo Ann. "It makes no sense ..."

Gilpin attempted to remain nonchalant, but he couldn't resist the urge to shoot a meaningful glance at Jake before posing his next question. "Did they say who this new witness was?"

"Yes. Apparently it was the guy who was driving the bus ..."

33

Summer in the City

The early months of that summer just zoomed by, with Jake preoccupied by a new wrinkle at work, and Jo Ann settling in to her new summer job slinging beer at the Coulson. No matter what, they remained inseparable, with Jo Ann becoming more and more of a fixture at the apartment Jake shared with Foley. Fortunately they all got along—Foley soon came to enjoy Jo Ann's company almost as much as he did Jake's. They were both such strapping, healthy-looking youngsters, that, it sometimes seemed to Foley, they might have come from another planet. They were, in fact, the product of several generations of Sudbury inbreeding that had resulted from company strictures on hiring—strict height and weight requirements were rigorously enforced—with the result that the residents of the Nickel Range tended to be taller and more athletic than elsewhere, or so it seemed to Foley. Never in his life had he felt like such a short person as he did here, though at five nine he was at least of average height. Yet whenever he went out in public in Sudbury he was invariably the shortest man in the room.

For Jake the early weeks of that summer went by in a blur because of a new challenge that was presented to him out at Frood—induction into the mine's rescue team. An elite group handpicked from among a group of volunteers, Mine Rescue team members were schooled in the basics of a host of professions, blending the skills of firefighters with hard rock mining, and even those of a paramedic. They were taught how to use highly specialized equipment like Scott Air-Paks—a self-contained breathing apparatus that featured pressurized oxygen pumped into a tight-fitting helmet. The gear was bulky, heavy and not overly comfortable, but it allowed Mine Rescue to safely enter dangerous areas of a mine where a fire had consumed all the oxygen or where a failure in the ventilation system had left pockets of dead—and potentially lethal—air. Such emergencies were exceedingly rare, but Jake and his fellow team members were capable of daring, and at times dangerous, rescue missions that could save the life of a fellow miner.

The training itself was physically gruelling, and Jake was ordered to climb a dizzying series of ladders, often carrying great weight, over daunting vertical distances. Besides the considerable weight of the miner's daily garb there was also the bulky Air Pak, and its air hose, valves and helmet. And then there was the additional weight strapped to him to simulate the dead weight of an inanimate body being hauled through a smoke-clogged drift or up ladders in a manway.

But Jake relished the challenge and the camaraderie of the team. No little prestige attached to joining an elite group of first responders trained to save lives in the most hostile environment imaginable. Morale and skill was kept razor sharp by a series of annual contests pitting Mine Rescue teams against one another, first within Inco and then against the best teams from other mining companies across Northern Ontario.

It all meant he often arrived home after work utterly exhausted, but Jake knew that his father and uncles, veteran miners all, were immensely proud that he had made it onto the Mine Rescue team.

Besides, there was always the distinct possibility that Jake might some day save a life with his newly won skills. That just such an opportunity would present itself so soon, and so close to home, Jake never imagined.

34

To Catch a Killer (II)

Foley discovered the transit bus drivers were out on strike—they had been organized by Mine Mill into Local 902—which made his job just that much easier. He approached the picket line, identified himself as a reporter, and asked for the picket captain. He was waved toward a tallish, portly bespectacled man wearing a white t-shirt that had the words "Mine Mill and Proud" emblazoned in blue on the back. Once again Foley identified himself, and he began to chat up the strike leader. After what he hoped was an interval of small talk sufficient to disguise his true interest, Foley asked casually whether the driver who'd been involved in that unfortunate accident downtown last summer happened to be out on picket duty that day?

The picket captain nodded, and pointed Gilpin toward yet another striker. Gilpin fished out his notepad and approached the man, who solemnly affirmed that he was indeed the driver Gilpin was seeking.

The reporter dissembled, hoping once again to disguise his true purpose, and asked the bus driver if they could sit down together and discuss the unfortunate accident over coffee in a more private setting. Gus's Restaurant, perhaps?

Gus's was a more private venue than a picket line, but only just. The popular coffee shop was a beehive of activity at lunch hour. With its location just up Elm Street from the courthouse—an interval that was heavily lined with law offices—Gus's was often packed with the city's most notorious gossips: its lawyers. The interior layout did little to enhance privacy, with a row of comfortable, low-sided booths running up the centre of the room. Foley and his interview subject slid comfortably into one such booth. It was an instant's inattention to his surroundings that would nearly cost Gilpin his life.

"So you were saying you were driving your bus downtown the day of the accident," the newspaperman prompted after laying his notebook and pen out on the table top, which was still moist from being freshly wiped down.

"Oh, it was no accident, mister, believe me. Someone wanted that poor man dead …"

"*What?* Why do you sat that?"

"Because he was pushed in front of my bus, plain as day."

"Really! And you know this how, exactly?"

"Because I seen it happen! One minute he wasn't there, and the next thing you know, there he was, right in front of me!"

"And did you get a look at who pushed him?" Foley suppressed his mounting excitement.

The driver nodded. "Sure did. The front windows a' them buses is mighty big, ya know, and we're sitting high up there in the catbird seat, we don't miss much."

"What did he look like, this man who did the pushing?"

"Big feller. Tall and fair-haired, with a crewcut, Looked like an ex-soldier, maybe."

Gilpin swallowed hard and nodded, trying hard not to betray the jolt of adrenalin that had just hit his system. "Do you think you could identify this individual if you ever saw him again?"

"Oh, most definitely. You don't forget a thing like that. Doesn't happen every day, thank God."

"And you told all this to the police?"

The driver shrugged and held his hands out, palms up as he looked at Foley with a look of wide-eyed disbelief. "They never even asked me! Chalked it all up as an accident. Nobody ever did talk to me about it 'til that insurance fella last week. And now you."

So stunned was Gilpin that he stopped taking notes, and he still failed to notice the Nosey Parker in the booth right behind them. He had not noticed Henry Hoople, nor recognized the man who had taken a poke at him in the Mine Mill Hall some months before, as Hoople slid furtively out of his own booth. All of a sudden he had urgent business back at the Hall ...

Hoople barged straight into McAdoo's office which was, as usual, wreathed in the blue smoke of a freshly lit cigar.

"You'll never guess who I just seen over at Gus's," Hoople announced.

"Oh yeah?" McAdoo closed the file he'd been reading and looked up at Hoople, who was in the Hall on grievances.

"Remember that little Commie prick reporter who was always hanging out with the old gang?"

"Oh, you mean old Fuzzy Gasbag?" McAdoo laughed. It had been some time since he'd had occasion to use the derisive nickname they'd assigned to Foley Gilpin.

"Yeah, that's him," Hoople affirmed with a laugh. "I think he was talking to one of the transit boys, grillin' him about that company guy who got himself run over by a bus last summer, remember him?"

"Yeah, Henry, sure I do." McAdoo reached for a pen and paper. "So what'd old Fuzzy want to know?"

Josef Stoptych was impressed. Most potential tenants who applied to live in the building left him cold—too many long hairs out there these days. The landlord was suspicious of their shaggy locks and slovenly ways, figuring if they were ever given half a chance to skip out on the rent they'd take it, and leave him holding the bag. But this newcomer was different. No long hair for him. With his blonde hair and crew-cut and clear, blue-eyed gaze he reminded Stoptych of the Waffen SS troopers he'd known during the war. Oh, they'd gained a bad reputation since VE Day, but the landlord secretly believed it was a bad rap—the result of propaganda spewed out by the Jews and Communists, mainly. Like many residents of Silesia,

Stoptych had managed to support all four sides during the war—the Nazis, the Red Army, the Allies, the Partisans—whoever had gained the temporary upper hand in the fighting that raged back and forth over his homeland, that benighted corner of Eastern Europe where Poland, Germany and the Ukraine overlapped.

When the war ended, Stoptych had escaped his homeland at the first opportunity, landing in an Austrian refugee camp where he'd been recruited to emigrate to Canada, with the proviso that he move to a Northern Ontario mining town called Sudbury where, he was assured, his employment application at a big mining company named Inco would be expedited and he'd immediately be granted secure, highly paid employment. In return he was expected to join the union at Inco and help combat the Reds who were secretly using the union to subvert Canadian democracy. It was a struggle Stoptych, who loathed Communists almost as much as he hated Jews, was only too happy to join—and he was not alone. The refugee camps of post-war Europe had proved fertile ground for Western companies and agencies eager to gain fresh recruits in the global struggle against Communism. The Americans, led by the Office of Strategic Services, forerunner of the CIA, had combed through the camps seeking not common labourers like Stoptych, but high-end scientists like Werner von Braun, who had helped Hitler develop the V2 rocket, and whose knowledge and skill with ballistics might prove useful to the Americans' own Cold War missile development program.

Josef Stoptych and the scores like him who were sponsored into Canada because of their pro-fascist, anti-Communist leanings were welcomed with open arms in Sudbury, where they were quickly integrated into the swarm of displaced persons who flooded into the city after the war.

So diverse was the city linguistically and ethnically that it billed itself as "the little League of Nations." But it was hardly a harmonious whole. Many of the newcomers had discreet, albeit hardcore, pro-fascist leanings which were at odds with their fellow countrymen. These differences, whether ideological, linguistic or ethnic, were often exploited by the company in a divide-and-conquer campaign designed to weaken the Mine Mill union internally. Where once there had been mainly so-called "Red Finns" now there were "White Finns" to counter their influence. Croats arrived to offset Serbs, and "Red Ukrainians" faced off against "White Ukrainians." The splits were soon felt on the job, where Croat glared at Serb over the lunchroom table, and they quickly spilled over into the community, where a dual system of ethnic clubs—each with its own hall—proliferated. All of these rivalling groups joined—and generally looked down upon—a large French-Canadian population that was equally divided between staunch, conservative rural anti-Communist Catholics and even stauncher rough, tough Mine Mill union supporters. These conflicting allegiances were bred in the bone, and would outlast the Cold War, as would the bricks and mortar of their respective meeting halls.

Canada, and Inco, kept their respective promises to Stoptych. He had indeed found gainful and highly lucrative employment. By dint of hard work—toiling every overtime shift that was offered—combined with frugal devotion to his own personal savings program, Stoptych had soon saved enough to seek an investment outlet for his nest egg. Like many of his fellow workers, he elected to invest in Sudbury real estate by buying several apartment buildings.

Now, for whatever reason, Josef Stoptych had a good feeling about the clean-cut newcomer with the clear blue eyes ...

35

The Old Provo's Trick

He extracted the matchbook thoughtfully from his pocket, and then, with one hand, he thumbed the cover open and bent a single match out of the pack, back and over the striker. It was an old provo's trick, this simple method of starting a fire. No accelerant—always a dead giveaway to the fire marshals who would later investigate the scene—was needed. And the fire would start, gently, gradually, and slowly, giving him time to get away safely, and the fire itself would consume this innocent, inert pack of matches, leaving no trace of the point of ignition.

He smiled at the simple beauty of the thing before placing the flaming matchbook atop the stack of newspapers on the wooden table and leaving the apartment, being careful to close the door behind him.

The apartment on the floor below was fully engulfed when Jake arrived home at the end of the afternoon shift. His first thought was of Jo Ann, who was, thankfully, still at work. He ran up the stairs without thinking, and found his apartment filled with the smoke rising from below.

His Mine Rescue training kicked in, and Jake instinctively dropped to his knees to crawl into Foley's bedroom. He had no idea how much smoke Foley had already inhaled, so Jake placed a hand over Foley's face, and only then did his friend begin to cough and sputter, rousing finally from a deep sleep.

"Foley! Foley! It's me, Jake!" He spoke with quiet intensity. "Listen, the place is on fire, we gotta get outta here!" And with that he unceremoniously dragged Foley bodily out of bed, still entangled in bedclothes. He grabbed one of his friend's hands and hitched it to his belt. The smoke was already thickening, a nasty, acrid effluvia that scorched his nose and throat. His eyes were tearing up badly and his nose was running, but it hardly mattered. The evil black smoke was now so thick he couldn't see anyway. Leading the way, Jake crawled on all fours, groping toward Foley's bedroom door, forcing himself to resist the urge to give way to the desperation and panic that clutched at him, as cloying as the acrid, stinking air that was filling his lungs, a lethal chemical stew of burning newspapers, lead-based paints and melting plastic electrical insulation from the apartment below.

The stairs were harrowing, with both Jake and Foley, still forced to remain on all fours, rolling and tumbling by way of descent. Finally both men crawled out the front door of the building. The intense heat of the blaze had blown out the windows of the apartment below theirs, and flames licked out hungrily against the night sky, illuminating Jake's desperate attempts to get his friend breathing again. Once again his membership on the Mine Rescue team paid off for Jake as he set to work performing emergency resuscitation on Gilpin. It took a while, but eventually the older man began to cough and sputter, chest heaving as he gasped for breath in the cool freshness of the night air. Relieved, Jake paused in his ministrations. He was still on his knees over Foley's prostrate form as he looked up at the angry flames as they shot fire out the windows above. Even here, down below, Jake couldn't quite clear his seared lungs of the stench of the toxic chemical soup they'd both been forced to inhale for far too long. Finally Jake forced himself to lie down on the ground beside Foley. As the adrenalin rush subsided Jake began to focus on his own breathing, inhaling lungfuls of the cool, fresh night air around him, exhaling, he hoped, the chemically laced smoky air that had almost killed them both. But the taste of it was still in his mouth, like a bad, and far too recent, memory. The sky above him was beginning to spin wildly and Jake thought he might pass out, but then he heard sirens from the direction of downtown, a scant half-dozen blocks away.

"Hey! Hey buddy! You okay?" Jake felt someone tugging roughly at his shirt. "Yeah, he's alive over here, Mike! They both are! Seem to be okay! Hey buddy! Is there anyone else in the building?"

Jake tried to respond—*wanted* to respond—but he felt mired in some slow-mo quicksand. It was just too much effort, and the truth was he didn't know. Finally he mustered the energy to lift his arms and hands, palms up, in a helpless gesture signalling the feeblest ignorance. The firefighter standing impatiently above him got the message. "Yeah, yeah, okay buddy, you don't know, I get it. Just take it easy now."

"Hey, Mike! Buddy here doesn't know if there's anybody still in there or not!" For Jake then, still lying flat on his back, the world was a simple place of two contending halves: half angry red, shot through with yellow flames licking hungrily into the other half, the peaceful infinite blackness of the night sky. And then the black won.

36

The Man Who Never Was

To Foley Gilpin the Sudbury police department had long since become a closed book—surly, mistrustful and uncommunicative in the extreme.

The sentiment was quite reciprocal: from the Chief on down, the entire department saw him coming, saw the portly, aging reporter as a well-known sympathizer of the old guard, hardcore Mine Mill, which made him a Communist sympathizer at the very least, an outright Commie at worst.

Gilpin encountered no such obstacles with the Office of the Ontario Fire Marshal, however. Whether it was the *Globe*'s well known pro-Tory leanings or the fact that the OFI was based in the Ontario Fire Marshal's Office in the provincial capital of Toronto, which was buffered by some three hundred miles from the incestuous, internecine Cold War politics of small-city Sudbury, Gilpin was never quite sure. But he suspected that his paper's pro-Tory editorial stance made all the difference to a provincial government where the Conservative Party had been comfortably ensconced for decades. It was an irony Gilpin rather relished: on the rough-and-tumble, rather hickish frontier of the Nickel Range he was regarded as an outlaw, but in Queen's Park-Bay Street Toronto, that bastion of private school, Tory Blue cronyism, which was the seat of the financial and political power that ruled the vast inland empire that was Ontario, he was a safe, rather tame, scribbler—an insider. (And it was *vast*. Out of the idle curiosity that made him such a good reporter, Gilpin had one day compared the size of Ontario to the state of Texas; he discovered to his amazement that the Canadian province was more than *seven times* as large as the outsized American state, and contributed a goodly share of the globe's total annual output of nickel and copper, yes, but also of gold and silver and platinum, as well as milled lumber and pulp and paper, and, to Gilpin's surprise, of agricultural products as well.)

For whatever reason, his call was promptly returned, and Gilpin was greeted rather warmly by the specialist dispatched to investigate the fire that had nearly killed him.

"We're classing the fire as suspicious, at the moment," he confided to Gilpin.

"But do you know where it started?"

The investigator nodded. "In the second floor apartment, directly below yours."

"What about *how* it started?"

The investigator hesitated, reaching for the file in front of him. "On that, we're not so sure … There was no trace of any accelerant of any kind, or any clear point of origin …"

"Yet you're still classing the fire as suspicious. Why is that?"

The investigator shrugged. "The tenant was absent when the fire began, which always makes us suspicious ..."

"Yes, and who was the tenant?"

"Funny thing is we don't really know ... He was new, apparently. Hadn't even moved his personal belongings in yet, which arouses further suspicion ..."

"But surely our landlord must have some kind of record?"

The investigator nodded in agreement, and flipped through his file once again. "You'd think. Josef Stoptych, yes, here it is. Claims he rented the place out to this new tenant based purely on sight alone ... because he liked the *look* of this guy."

"Which was?"

"Clean-cut, not some kind of hippie. Tall, blonde, athletic build. Maybe ex-military."

"Will you take this to the police?"

"Can't, I'm afraid—there's no proof a crime was actually committed. And no trace of this mystery tenant ... He never got a phone, Stoptych got no references and he paid the rent in cash, first and last. And now he's gone with the wind."

"Almost like he never existed."

"Exactly."

37

The Go-Go Boys

On the job Jake was still at Frood, in an area remarkable for the pace of technological change it was undergoing. Already Jake and Bob were using the second generation three-boom jumbo drill, a considerable improvement over the original, which had been deemed a spectacular success on all fronts. Bob and Jake easily made their daily, oversized push—and with the expenditure of far less energy. And the mechanized drill made the job safer—the thing could be walked out past the end of the screening overhead and be left to drill off the rounds automatically—if the back caved in, only a machine would be buried, rather than a man on a jackleg.

The company was happy, too. Bob and Jake's productivity doubled and doubled again, and plans were already underway to introduce more jumbos, not only in other headings at Frood, but in the company's other mines, as well.

And other parts of the vision Bob had outlined for Jake were coming to pass, too. New, diesel-powered trackless mucking machines, known as scoop trams, were introduced into the new, more spacious stopes carved out by the jumbos. Massive, powerful machines built low to the ground, the scoop trams ran on huge, solid-rubber tires that were sometimes taller than a man. These roaring behemoths were graded by the cubic volume of their buckets, which lifted the muck out of the heading and carried it to the ore pass. The smallest scoop, the ST-2, had a two cubic yard bucket and was dwarfed by the ST-8, the largest scoop tram in use.

As a result of all this the Frood Mine Lower Country had become a much noisier, much faster-moving place, with the headlights of scoop trams zipping to and fro and the manic pounding of the jumbos, three steels turning at once, each squirting its own stream of water out of the drillholes. The volume of ore drilled, blasted and mucked out increased exponentially, and with it, bonus earnings.

With all this frenetic activity the newly mechanized parts of Frood Mine were soon dubbed the "go-go areas." Jake and Bob were among the very first go-go boys. Bob was enthralled by the labour-saving devices, thankful for the wear-and-tear they saved on his aging frame. His younger partner, meanwhile, wasn't so sure. Something about the whole thing continued to niggle at Jake, something he couldn't quite put his finger on …

38

A Fire in the Dark

Even with the labour-saving jumbos, Jake and Bob still finished their shifts bathed in sweat, their overalls soaked beneath their oilers, the heavy water-proof slickers favoured by many miners to ward off the endless drizzle of the underground workings. The reason: here in the Lower Country they were closer than ever to the underground fire that stubbornly resisted every effort to extinguish it and that was fast becoming an accepted, if enervating, fact of life in Frood Mine's Lower Country. They tried every stratagem—pouring water to it, starving it of oxygen—that mine managers and engineers could conceive. But in the end, it was a standoff—that portion of the mine was simply walled off with a bulkhead, and the fire was left to smolder, in the hope it would eventually consume all its fuel and snuff itself out. Burn, baby, burn. But it would continue to smoulder for decades, becoming a part of Sudbury's underground lore, pulsing and glowing, unseen there in the absolute darkness of the belly of the mine. It was a mute reminder—and perhaps a reproach—of the folly that men can enter a place where it was never intended they should go; and in their greed and technological reach and insatiable craving for more and more and ever more, they would contrive the conceit that they could safely ignore the cosmic, karmic consequences of their actions.

39

Jake's Last Shift

It happened at the end of another steamy, sweat-soaked shift, vexed by one of the drill's booms stubbornly refusing to turn as rapidly as the others—a glitch in the hydraulics, perhaps—and so Jake left Bob behind to walk the defective machine to the service garage and to report the problem to supervision and the incoming cross-shift.

Jake was making his way alone along the main haulage drift on the way out to the cage—an uneventful passage—until he reached the unmarked divide between the future of mining and the past. And it was just there, as he trudged wearily out of the go-go area into the older, tracked portion of the level that he first noticed the tail lights of a train of ore cars on the track in the far-off distance. But even from his vantage point hundreds of feet away, Jake could sense something was wrong. The red lights appeared immobile, instead of receding into the distance at a faster pace than the tired, sweat-soaked Jake was walking. No, clearly the string of loaded ore cars wasn't moving, and that was odd.

As he approached the ore train Jake saw the motor was at a dead stop, and that the motorman had descended from his loco to wrestle with one of the cars in the middle of his train. By the time he had drawn even with the stalled train, Jake was finally able to discern the nature of the problem: one of the wheels on one of the train's middle cars had jumped the track, threatening to cause a chain reaction that would drag the cars behind it off the track, thus derailing the whole train.

The motor man, Jake can see, is a young guy—even younger than himself—and clearly uncertain as to what to do next.

"Need a hand?"

"Yeah, I guess." The youngster regards Jake with a worried look. Even a greenhorn knows the seriousness of the situation: left unmoved, the partially derailed train will clog up the haulage drift, eventually backing up all further traffic on the line, and, finally, shutting down all production in this portion of the level. One wheel on one ore car is creating a million dollar snafu that could well cost the young motor man his new job.

Jake's cap lamp bobs as he nods in sympathy with his co-worker.

"Got anything to pry with?"

This time it's the youngster's turn to nod as he produces a ten foot scaling bar that he's somehow obtained from—somewhere. A sturdy instrument, indeed. Jake is impressed.

"Good. Okay, you start wedging over there on your side, and I'll take the low side over here. You push it towards me, and I'll push it back towards you. That way we rock it up high enough to get it back up on the track. Got it?"

"Yes sir."

Jake feels a momentary pang at being called "sir," as if he has just entered a new, and not entirely welcoming, country. Something tells him it will happen again.

"All right. On my count of three. One ... two ... three!"

The car full of muck is crazily heavy, as Jake had known it would be, and at first Jake is just able to turn its momentum by bracing his legs and thrusting back against the top of the car with both hands. But, after a momentary period when they rock the swaying, heavily laden car in rough equilibrium, things begin to go horribly wrong. Jake realizes, too late, that he has failed to reckon with this new, younger partner's strength and enthusiasm—fuelled, no doubt by his eagerness to get his assigned task completed successfully—or the way they would both be compounded by the leverage the kid could muster with his makeshift pry bar. Jake averts disaster at first by straining to the utmost to check the momentum of the car as it sways towards him. But Jake's own kinetic energy is soon turned against him as the kid braces the scaling bar to shorten the arc of the swing on his side. This is a manoeuvre they both understand—or think they do—one they've both employed dozens of times before: rocking a vehicle back and forth in ever greater oscillations to free it from a snowbank. The technique requires increasing momentum, plus the vehicle's own motive power, in steady rhythm, to work. But here the only momentum is created by the exertions of the two men. Jake is bracing for the strain once again when it happens: the momentum of the swaying car combined with the pull of gravity is more than Jake can handle. Everything that happens then happens in slow motion—Jake sees the heavy car rocking toward him, strains to slow its approach, is overmastered by its sheer weight and momentum, and watches in horror as it begins to tip toward him, spilling the jagged heavy muck over him, slowly at first, and then with shuddering, bone-crushing speed.

"Shit!" Jake is pinned feet first by the rough flow of ore. Still straining fruitlessly against the weight of the overturning car, Jake is twisted to his left by the car's contents, which bury him, first to his knees, then up to his waist, before knocking him down entirely and out of sight to his erstwhile partner.

"Hey!"

"Hey buddy!" The kid, alarmed by Jake's sudden disappearance, comes running around the tail end of the stalled train. He arrives breathless, standing over Jake, clearly appalled at what he sees. "Oh man! Are you all right?"

Jake is lying on one side, buried up to his neck in muck. He can only see the kid with one eye, and even that is blurry because he can't turn his neck to see, and the kid is just at the outer edge of his limited peripheral vision. Anger wells up in Jake, but he suppresses the urge to snap at the kid. *Do I look like I'm all right? What the fuck? Go get some help to get me outta here!*

The kid swallows hard, Adam's apple bobbing. At least there is no blood. None that he can see, anyway. He fights back the panic that is sweeping over him like a wave. "Okay! Listen, I'm gonna run for help, get some more guys to help dig you outta there! Okay? I'll be right back!"

And with that the kid is gone, pelting down the drift toward the shaft, running awkwardly in his big steel toes, his hard hat bouncing crazily on his head.

Jake's vision is limited to the feeble cone of light from his cap lamp so he hears, rather than sees, the kid disappearing down the drift. After that he is alone, lying on his side, very nearly buried alive in high grade Frood Mine muck. That Frood Mine high grade Jake knew so well. Its faintly greenish cast. Muck so rich, so coveted, that it yearned to transmute itself into precious and base metal, wanting only air, provided by the miners themselves as they drilled and blasted their way into the ore body, and a little fuel in the form of old, square set timbers, to spontaneously combust and begin the reduction process, as it had in the fire that smouldered even now somewhere in the mine deep below Jake's prostrate, twisted form.

He knows he should turn off his cap lamp, to preserve the precious, dwindling supply of electricity remaining in the battery strapped to his hip, but he cannot reach the small, finely gnarled knob attached to the cap lamp mounted on his hard hat. His left arm is pinned beneath him, and his right arm is buried just deeply enough that he can't move it, either.

Gradually Jake becomes aware that he has no sensation below his waist. *I can't feel my legs! Christ! What's going on down there?* The turn of events has been so sudden that only now is the seriousness of his situation sinking in to Jake. *What if my legs are broken or—God forbid—even crushed? How will I ever be able to mine again? Or walk, or make love to Jo Ann?"* And, for the first time, Jake feels a surge of panic beginning to well up in his throat. *Breathe!* he tells himself ... *Just breathe!* He forces himself to concentrate on just that, on drawing one good inhalation through his nose, into his lungs, but this, too, is impossible with the ore spilled so tightly around him, packed close to his chest and back. There is simply no room for his chest to expand. This realization triggers an even stronger wave of panic until some even more primal instinct for self-preservation takes over and Jake tries, instead, breathing shallow, modest volumes of air through his mouth. *That works.* His gratitude is so profound that, with his mouth barely a centimetre off the floor of the drift, the taste of sulphur, rock dust and mine damp is almost a welcome thing.

Next he becomes aware of the quiet. Not absolute silence, certainly—back towards the go-go area he hears, far off in the distance, the revving and roaring of the scoop trams and the rumble of muck dropping through the ore passes. He is also aware, in the silence, of the ringing in his ears that has now become such an ever-present thing that he barely hears it. But now, helpless beneath the muck, he concentrates on the ringing. It has, he decides, become louder since his first shift underground. Hard to believe that was just over a year ago! The year has gone past in a flash, so much has happened. But now time has slowed to a crawl. *Christ! Where is my own Mine Rescue crew? How long have I been here? Not sure how much longer I can stand this! Huh! Not like I have much choice* … And then, from the direction of the loading station he hears it, a low-geared motor whining at high revs to make maximum speed—the man car, almost certainly. Soon enough he sees its headlights throwing shadows on the walls of the drift, and then here it is, with guys hanging off it every which way.

"There he is!"

The motor slows to a stop, is switched off, and Jake is surrounded by his co-workers. They quickly size up the situation, as if determining a plan of attack.

"Jesus, McCool! The whole idea is we put the muck into the cars, not the other way around! Didn't Jesperson teach ya nothing?"

Jake recognizes the voice of Jeff "Sniper" Robertson.

"Ha, ha. Very funny, Sniper. Now will you please get this shit the fuck offa me?"

Before Robertson has time to crack off again Jake hears the sound of the chunks being lifted and thrown back into the ore car, sometimes shattering on the side of the car. The rescue party sets to its task with a will. The sound of muck being moved, and heavy breathing. Some of the larger chunks, Jake knows, are very, very heavy. It will take two guys just to budge them, much less lift them.

"Hey! I see a leg! I got a leg here! Okay, now, be very careful guys."

The last of the muck is being gingerly lifted off Jake's right leg. His resurrection has begun. It continues for several more minutes as chunks of varying sizes are carefully removed from his right hip, his arm, and at last one hand is free. Jake slowly wiggles his fingers at first. His right hand is badly bruised, but it works. Next he makes a few tentative motions with his arm. So far, so good. The muck is plucked, piece by piece, from around his torso. At last Jake can breathe. The air in his lungs has never felt so sweet. "Phew. Okay, fellas, I think I'm gonna be all right, if I could just sit up …"

Half a dozen strong arms are extended to Jake's upraised arm in an effort to pull him upright, but it's too soon. His left arm and half-buried torso resist all their efforts.

"Nope, no good fellas." Jake feels the arms straining against his relent. "We're gonna have to dig him all the way out." And they do, chunk by chunk, piece by piece, until Jake's resurrection is complete, and he is pulled, wobbly, to his feet. But he collapses. Is pulled back on to his feet again. Collapses again.

"Whoa! This just ain't workin'! Okay, fellas, let's just walk him on over to the man car there …" And they do, Jake's arms wrapped around the necks of two of his rescuers, his feet dragging across the deck, until he is hefted safely onto the man car, which delivers him to the cage, which has been has summoned to the level to make an emergency evacuation.

And so ends Jake's last shift.

Everyone from the level is so densely packed against Jake in the cage that he barely needs his legs to remain upright. He is, for once, almost grateful for the fusty, sweaty crush of bodies which has become such a familiar part of his underground working day.

On surface the light of day, even filtered through the lofty gloom of the headframe, is more glaring than ever, and it feels like everyone is staring at Jake as he staggers past on his way into the dry. Once there, he is greeted by a strange sight, almost an apparition. In the middle of the large room, which is wreathed in a cloud of hot shower steam, a solitary figure sits on the floor atop the central drain. The grey water pouring off a hundred filthy miners' naked bodies swirls around him as he nonchalantly soaps his own grimy body. Jake frowns, and shakes his head in disbelief. He motions at the sitting figure as if to say "What the fuck?"

"Charley Burrell," whispers a workmate.

Jake nods, looking down again at the man on the floor, half hidden by shower mist. He knows old Charley's story well. A hotshot bonus miner from the 1930s, Charley had once been a man of prodigious strength and skill. He'd earned a king's ransom in bonus, it was said, investing it balls-in in local real estate. On the verge of becoming a millionaire, Charley was wiped out in the Great Depression. His health had been ruined in forty years underground, but severe arthritis and white-hand syndrome had not felled the stubborn Burrell. Convinced a return to his golden bonus earning days lay just before him, Charley stubbornly resisted the company's repeated efforts to move him into a light duty job on surface. Still, despite everything, Charley is still capable of a day's work underground, but only just—the day's efforts leave him too exhausted to shower standing up, a deficiency his co-workers choose to ignore out of love and respect for this once-powerful, still legendary and prideful, old man. But why, Jake wonders, has he not witnessed this bizarre scene before? It is a sight he will never forget.

And at last Jake emerges into the languid swelter of a Sudbury summer's eve. He is staggered by the smell, so mysterious and so sweet, and by the sound of a million crickets tuning up for the summer night ahead.

Jake stops and takes a deep breath of the rich, earthy aroma. It has never smelled so sweet. He summons every last ounce of strength and, limping only slightly, Jake McCool heads for the parking lot.

He will never work another shift underground ever again.

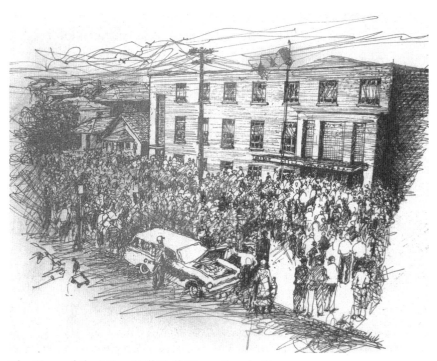

The Siege of the Mine Mill Hall (Oryst Sawchuk)

Acknowledgements

I am indebted to a number of true-life characters who helped this fictional account of imaginary characters come to life on the printed page. First and foremost are my technical advisors Peter Miner, Tommy Raftery and the other members of the Mine Mill/UNIFOR Local 598 Retirees, who provided invaluable input about working underground and the history of the Mine Mill-Steel Raids. Two now deceased former leaders of Local 598, the late Mike Solski and Jim Tester, were especially formative in my thinking about the period. I miss them both terribly. I am also hugely indebted to Oryst Sawchuk, who very generously donated his artwork to the project. His painting "Hardrock" graces the cover. A framed print of the original hangs above me now as it did throughout the writing of this book, providing a kind of visual, creative inspiration that reflects the unique nature of our hometown. Artist, architect, activist, designer, entrepreneur and last of the old time ladies' men, Oryst, like his art, is a unique Sudbury creation. Friends Phil Taylor in Toronto and Paul de la Riva in Sudbury also played special roles in guiding The Raids into print, as did Robin Philpot of Baraka

Books of Montreal. In the latter I seem to have found, quite unexpectedly, a soul mate.

As always I was guided in the creation of *The Raids* by my long-time, steadfast and brilliant agent, Janine Cheeseman of Aurora Artists in Toronto. Her patience with and attention to an aging Sudbury scribbler whose business will, I fear, never prove especially lucrative is a special gift I will always appreciate.

Also instrumental in the early gestation of this book was my old friend and colleague Jack Todd of Montreal, who provided sound advice and kind encouragement when *The Raids* was still inchoate.

Another invaluable resource was Marthe Brown, Head Archivist of the J.N. Desmarais Library at Sudbury's Laurentian University. Always just a phone call away, Marthe is, like me, a transplanted Sudburian drawn to the irresistible lure of the city's singular labour history. She has since become a foremost expert on the subject.

Finally but by no means last, there is the closest of all the concentric circles that aided in the creation of this book, my family, foremost among them being my beautiful wife Anita Yawney Lowe, to whom the work is dedicated. A proud Sudbury girl born and bred, she puts the "class" back in working class. Her sharp eye spotted several anachronisms that, had they found their way into print, would have proved highly embarrassing. And then there is my own marketing mini-team, my daughters Julia and Melanie Lowe along with family friend Ian MacDonald. The kids are all right.

Like all creators of historical fiction, I have striven to stay astride the razor's edge, maintaining the delicate, and sometimes lacerating, balance between pure fiction and historical narrative. My goal throughout has been to maintain historical and technical accuracy while avoiding anachronism. The test has been verisimilitude, while avoiding slavish repetition of the pure historical narrative. To the degree that I have succeeded I am indebted to the aforementioned cast of helpful characters. Any shortcomings and failings are all my own.

-ML

Sudbury, February, 2014

MORE FROM BARAKA BOOKS

FICTION

I Hate Hockey
François Barcelo

Principals and Other Schoolyard Bullies
Short Stories by Nick Fonda

Washika, A Novel
Robert A. Poirier

Hell Never Burns
The Adventures of Radisson 1
Martin Fournier

NONFICTION

Rwanda and the New Scramble for Africa
From Tragedy to Useful Imperial Fiction
Robin Philpot

Slouching Towards Sirte
NATO's War on Libya and Africa
Maximilian Forte

Challenging the Mississippi Firebombers
Memories of Mississippi 1964-65
Jim Dann

Barack Obama and the Jim Crow Media
The Return of the Nigger Breakers
Ishmael Reed

An Independent Quebec
The Past, the Present and the Future
Jacques Parizeau

The Question of Separatism
Quebec and the Struggle over Sovereignty
Jane Jacobs

A People's History of Quebec
Jacques Lacoursière & Robin Philpot

The History of Montréal
The Story of a Great North American City
Paul-André Linteau